Hunt Me Down

Down

fight for me

A.L. JACKSON

A.L. Jackson
www.aljacksonauthor.com
Cover Design by RBA Designs
Photo by Focus and Blur
Editing by AW Editing
Formatting by Mesquite Business Services

Print ISBN: 978-1-946420-07-7
eBook ISBN: 978-1-946420-06-0

Hunt Me Down

More From A.L. Jackson

one

Broderick

'm not sure how you handle things where you come from, Mr. Wolfe, but I can assure you it is not how we handle things in Gingham Lakes. Mrs. Tindall has been a value to our small community since the fifties, and her family long before then, and I have every intention of securing that legacy for many years to come. Why don't you make things easier on yourself and remain in your high-rise office, which I'm sure affords you quite the dramatic view of Manhattan. You seem better suited for that than our 'provincial' town.

I didn't even fight the satisfied smile that pulled at my lips as I let my eyes retrace her latest email.

God, this woman was a handful.

Determined and feisty.

A challenge I couldn't wait to take on.

For the last five months, we'd been going back and forth via email. My interactions with this tough-as-nails attorney, who was working pro bono for a tiny company in an even tinier city in Alabama, had escalated with each click of *send*.

Maybe it was a little sick that I'd come to crave this game.

Cat and mouse.

Round and round.

She was sharp and obviously loyal. I'd never even seen her. But apparently, I didn't have to. Just sitting there and reading the fight in her words made my dick hard.

There was nothing like a strong woman who knew what she wanted.

The best part was I wanted it more.

My laptop screen burned through the dim light of my high-rise office, which did indeed offer the most spectacular view of Manhattan. With a smirk, I leaned forward and let my fingers fly across the keyboard.

That is where you're mistaken, Ms. Redd. I'm sure you're well aware of our company's reputation. The Wolfe name is the very definition of success. It's the cornerstone on which our company has been built, and I will not let that name be tarnished. I will have that building, and in the end, my hotel will stand in its place. I'm trying to be fair, but make no mistake, if you force me into a corner, I will come out, teeth bared. I've been told they're sharp.

A shock of lust curled in my gut as I sent the email. Why did I get the feeling I would love sinking my teeth into this woman?

It took only a few moments before my inbox pinged with a new message.

Is that a threat, Mr. Wolfe? Because if it is, I can assure you, my nails are equally as long, and I never hesitate to fight back.

Visions assaulted me. Ones of her nails clawing at my shoulders and raking down my back. Her body straining beneath mine as I ravaged her.

My breaths turned shallow as I typed out a response.

Is that a promise or your own threat, Ms. Redd? I'm *up* for either.

God. What the fuck did I think I was doing? I'd always been about the job. But this woman...this fiery woman had me stepping out of bounds. Saying things I knew I should never say.

Her response was almost immediate.

Don't flatter yourself. You're clearly compensating, and I definitely don't need that kind of disappointment. Save yourself the trip. You wouldn't want to embarrass yourself with that kind of *failure*.

"Oh, you went there, did you?" I murmured beneath my breath. I fucking loved that she didn't hold back. My teeth scraped my lower lip, my mouth watering as I gave into the chase.

Failure is not a part of my vocabulary, Ms. Redd. I think we've already established that. But don't worry, at the end of all of this, you will be thanking me.

I pressed send a little too eagerly, becoming even more excited when I clicked into her quick response.

Only in your lofty, lofty dreams, Mr. Wolfe. I will see to it those dreams are crushed.

A chuckle rumbled free, and I rubbed at my jaw. She had no idea just how much pleasure I would take in crushing her.

This could have been an easy acquisition.

We'd made a more than generous offer, after all. Instead of accepting it and moving on, they let nostalgia taint their decision and rejected the small fortune.

Some people didn't seem to understand when it was best to take the path of least resistance.

But you wouldn't see me complaining. They had no clue just

how much I relished the battle.

My cell bleeped and lit up where it rested on the glass desk, and I subdued the irritation that fought to work its way up my throat. I cleared it as I rocked forward and accepted the call.

"Father," I said by way of hello as I stood and shrugged into my suit jacket before closing down my laptop and sliding it into its leather case.

"Son. Tell me you've taken care of the issue."

"I'm working on it."

"Working on it isn't good enough. I needed this finished yesterday."

I gritted my teeth in an attempt to keep from spitting the words at him. "I told you, I would handle this one my way."

He huffed. "Haven't you figured out yet that *your* way doesn't work?"

A jolt of bitter laughter tripped from my tongue. "I think I've cleaned up enough of your messes that you would have realized by now that it does."

If it were up to my father, he would have gone in there and basically stolen that building right out from under that old lady. His men had no qualms about making a threat or two to get what he wanted, bending people to his will by cowardly shows of force.

Silence traveled the line, the two of us at odds, the constant contention that had churned between us since I was a little boy so close to reaching its boiling point.

"Two weeks, Broderick. Two weeks," he finally said. There was no missing the threat.

"I won't need them." My voice lowered. "And I'm warning you—do not interfere in this. I *will* do this my way."

"We'll see." That was the last thing he said before the line went dead.

Fuck. I squeezed the phone in my hand. It took every ounce of willpower I had not to send my phone sailing through the air.

Broderick Wolfe Sr. thought he was the epitome of success.

Believed his efforts were what Wolfe Industries was built upon.

When in truth, the man was nothing but underhanded deals and greed.

Those were footsteps I refused to walk in.

I worked relentlessly for what I wanted.

Chased it.

Hunted it until I had it in my clutches.

And when I won? It was because I was actually the best at what I did.

I buttoned a single button on my jacket and shook out the cuffs. Lifting my chin, I grabbed my case and strode out the door.

I had work to do.

And I was going to love every second of it.

two

Lillith

"So help me God, if he even looks at me wrong, I will snap. I think there's a legitimate chance someone will have to keep me from strangling him, Nikki. Gah…he's so infuriating." With my phone pressed to my ear, I tipped my face toward the sky and sucked in a few breaths of cold air as if it might stand the chance of cooling some of the anger still boiling in my blood.

Never had I hated a man as much as I hated Broderick Wolfe. That snarky, arrogant voice made my skin crawl. Of course, it was a voice I'd never actually heard. What was most frustrating was the fact that even in its silence it skated my skin like sex and sin.

No question, that was what this man was.

Sin.

Wicked and immoral.

Ten minutes ago, I'd left a meeting where we were planning exactly what strategy we'd take tomorrow when the big dogs from Wolfe Industries descended on our city.

I needed a few moments to vent.

My best friend Nicole laughed through the line. At least

someone found some humor in the situation. "Oh, I seriously doubt you're going to actually strangle him. You might have spent the last five months fantasizing about it, but I know you, Lily Pad, and you are the pillar of self-restraint. But if the stories are true and he's as gorgeous as everyone says he is, you have been fantasizing about all the wrong things."

The winter air was chilly, and I tightened the belt of my coat, my black patent heels clicking on the gray-bricked sidewalk that ran the quaint downtown street. I strode beneath the trees, their barren branches stretched over my head like a shield of protection. Rays of sunlight darted through the spindly limbs, creating a pattern of warmth on the ground.

Gorgeous old buildings rose up on each side of the street. Most of them were one-to-three stories high, the upper floors apartments and the bottom floors family-run and independent stores.

Many had been there since long before I was born.

So yes.

I could admit many were run down and in dire need of repair.

But that didn't make the histories held within their walls any less important.

Our city had always stood for something—family and community and coming together when things got rough.

There were parades on almost every holiday, and our parks and lakes were meticulously maintained—a safe place where children could run and play—all thanks to the residents who devoted their time and efforts to make sure the public areas were cared for. And when someone was in need? Those same residents came together with fundraisers and food drives to help ease the burden.

That was something I would do everything in my power to protect.

"Believe me, Nikki. There is absolutely no fantasizing on my part other than imagining his complete demise. The man is an arrogant slime ball. I don't care if he looks like Charlie Hunnam—I'm talking SOA here—I don't want anything to do with him other than to run him out of town as quickly as I can."

Nikki gasped as if it were the most horrific statement I'd ever made. "That is some serious hate, Lily. SOA? Are you sure you're really going there?"

I sighed, and a tumble of nerves rolled in my stomach as I approached the storefront at the heart of it all. My gaze traced the plate glass windows with the store's name and logo printed in white.

Tindall's Thimbles.

"You think that hate is undeserved?"

Nikki hesitated, and I could almost see her chewing furiously at the tip of her thumbnail, as if she weren't sure what to say. Her voice dropped. "Is there really anything wrong with revitalization? The city could use the jobs."

A sigh filtered free. "Of course we could use the jobs. But you know this is different. They're forcing this without consideration of the people who have been here all along. They're steamrolling people out of their homes and out of business without a second thought other than the number of dollars that will line their pockets. It's not as if they actually care about Gingham Lakes. You know the second they sign on the dotted line, they're out of here."

"You're probably right."

"If you were to read the emails I've shared with them, especially *him*, you'd understand, Nikki. This is all about the money. Any bullshit they're feeding us about pumping fresh blood into the community is just that—bullshit."

A tease made its way into her tone. "And we all know the bullshit stops with Lillith Redd."

Memories of when I couldn't see through people's bullshit barreled through me, and I pushed out the words on a whisper. "God, I hope so." I shook them off before I got too lost to them. "All right, I need to get inside."

"Okay, but I'll see you tonight at seven, right?"

Shit.

I'd forgotten about that.

"Of course," I muttered noncommittedly.

I could almost see Nikki raising her eyebrow at me. "Do not

bail on me, Lily Pad. You need to unwind. I don't care how busy you are or what you need to prepare for, you are getting a night out. Do you understand me?"

I puffed out a breath. "Fine. I'll be there."

"Promise?"

"Promise."

"Okay, see you then. Don't make me show up at your office to drag your ass out."

A short laugh rumbled free. "I wouldn't dream of it. I'll see you then."

"Bye."

I ended the call and slipped my cell into my bag. Sucking in a breath, I reached out and pulled open the door. A bell dinged from above, the light tinkle ushering in a thousand more memories.

The overwhelming relief I'd felt every time I'd stepped through this door.

The warmth and the comfort.

The hope when the only thing I'd felt was fear and defeat.

Movement pulled my attention to the far corner where an arch led to the back room filled with sewing machines and fabrics and tools. On the opposite side of the sewing machines were racks full of hanging garment bags waiting to be picked up by their brand new owners or to be reunited after a repair or tailor.

Addelaine all but floated out, the old woman willowy and thin. Hair long and silver. Grayed, blue eyes keen.

"Lillith, child," she murmured through a tender, wrinkled smile. "It's so wonderful to see you."

Immediately, I went to her, wrapped my arms around her frail body, and hugged her close. She smelled like baby powder and cotton, the way she always had.

"Addelaine," I whispered.

For a long moment, I clung to her before I forced myself to untangle from her familiar warmth. Even still, I reached out for one of her weathered hands. "Tell me how you're holding up? Has anyone been harassing you? Have you received any more letters?"

Softly, she smiled. "I couldn't be better."

A frown pulled at my brow. "You don't have to pretend for me, Addelaine. I can't imagine the type of stress this has put you under."

She touched my cheek. "Hmm…child…why do I get the feeling it's you who is the one who is stressed? I told you before, whatever will be, will be."

"And what will be is you staying put, right here, where you belong." The words were out, strength behind them. I wouldn't allow myself to fathom another outcome.

Her chuckle was slow as she worked her way back around the counter and began to sift through the orders she would start that day. "With you on my side? I have no doubt about that."

"They come in tomorrow." I glanced around the space. "The people who are trying to steal this building from you."

I knew she wanted to hide it, but I saw the resigned fear that flashed through her features. "It's going to be a fight."

"A fight we will win." I took an emphatic step forward. "We're fighting for what's right."

Her smile was sad. "I'm the one who got myself in this mess, Lillith. How many years am I behind on my taxes? And now the mortgage has gone late? I'm the one who hasn't been holding up to my end of the bargain. I took out that second mortgage thinking I'd be able to repay it, and you and I both know I just can't. Sometimes it's better to admit it's time to let things go."

If I had enough liquid cash, I would pay it off myself. But between the second mortgage and back taxes, the total was much more than I'd been able to get together. So, I'd settled on the one thing I could do—fight the battle through legal channels.

"Your family has been in this building for eighty years. You grew up here," I told her.

Meaningfully, she looked across at me. "And so did you."

I gulped around the emotion that threatened to seize my heart. "Yes." I took a pleading step forward. "You saved me, Addelaine. You took me in when I had nowhere else to go. And I won't stand for someone taking your home away from you, too."

I fumbled over the counter and took hold of her hand again. "I promise you, I will do whatever it takes to ensure that doesn't happen."

She squeezed back, her eyes raking my clothing, my dress pants and heels. But most of her attention was on the coat I wore. The thick, red material sewn to become something solid.

A patchwork of healing.

I could still feel the pain in my fingertips as I'd struggled to work a needle into the coarse, heavy material when I was fifteen. I could still hear Addelaine's voice in my ear as she'd coaxed me through it. Telling me all goals were achieved through some amount of pain.

When she'd whispered about growth and strength and had slowly but steadily helped to mold me into the woman I'd become.

She patted the back of my hand. "You're a good girl, Lillith. You will always be the granddaughter I never had. Whatever happens, know you have made me proud."

And that was exactly why I would do absolutely anything to make sure I didn't let her down.

three

Broderick

"What do you think?" James asked. He was my partner and my closest friend, and truly the only person in the world who I trusted wholly and without question.

"It looks solid to me."

"You're still confident?"

"Of course I'm still confident," I returned without hesitation. I was sure he already knew the answer. I was always confident.

"Your father is going to be pissed."

I scoffed. "When isn't he pissed?"

"Touché." James laughed quietly, and I could almost see him nodding. "All right then. Keep me posted after the meeting tomorrow. Good luck and let me know if you need anything."

"I will." After ending the call, I stuffed my cell in my jean's pocket and slowly ambled down the bustling street of downtown. Fairy lights were strung between the buildings, crisscrossing the busy road in the downtown area that ran the edge of the lake.

It was an area that had been reinvigorated over the last ten years. Life pumped back into its veins after the mill and cannery had shut down in the eighties.

A new kind of energy thrummed the street.

Vigorous and buzzing.

This was exactly what I hoped to achieve with the revitalization project just three miles away in the old town square that had once been the focal point of this city. The one mile radius was downtrodden but bursting with possibility.

And I was a guy who was all about possibility.

Pair it with opportunity, and my visions were unstoppable.

Earlier today, I'd driven through the area, checking out the exteriors of the building we still needed to acquire.

Excitement had burned like a fucking flame as I'd taken in the untapped potential.

Then I'd checked into my suite up the block, shed my suit, and redressed before I'd headed out into the approaching night. I wanted to take in the vibe of the locals out casting aside their day-to-day cares or maybe grumbling about them.

Sit back and watch. Get a read on exactly what we were working with.

I checked my phone again, a little disappointed that I hadn't gotten a reply from Ms. Redd after I'd invited her to meet me for drinks and whatever other activities that may arise.

Not that I'd expected her to accept.

I'd just been hoping she'd tell me to go to hell.

Maybe spar with me some more.

Amp me up to go toe to toe with her tomorrow afternoon.

My stomach tightened in anticipation. Fuck. I couldn't wait to be in a room with her. I'd forced myself not to look her up and, instead, let my imagination run wild, envisioning everything from a ditzy Elle Woods to an older hard-assed Diane Lockhart.

I just couldn't help myself. Sue me.

Just as I was approaching the intersection, my attention caught on a busy bar sitting on the corner. It was two stories high with an upstairs terrace. People leaned on the railing as they chatted and laughed, taking swigs of their beers and sipping their cocktails.

It was exactly what I was looking for.

Roughing an easy hand through my hair, I pulled open the door and stepped inside, gaze quick to scan the area.

Edison lights, which were strung from the high ceilings, hung down to add a glow to the dusky space. The floors were reclaimed wood, and the walls were old brick. It all added a comforting charm to the modern furniture and decorations that gave the vibe this was the place everyone wanted to be.

That was the ambiance I wanted to achieve for the whole town. A slice of exactly what I wanted to accomplish here—a merging of old and new.

It was a shame so many people were afraid of change.

Small groups sat around high-topped round tables, and more crowded the marble-topped bar. Muted laughter tumbled down from the staircase that led to the second floor and mingled with the mild chatter that echoed on the walls of the bottom floor.

I headed directly for the bar at the back and slid onto a free stool. I raised a hand to grab the bartender's attention.

He lifted his bearded chin at me. "What can I get you, man?"

I scanned the top shelf.

"Knob Creek. Neat."

"You sound like a man who needs to unwind. Bad day?"

I rubbed at my chin. "Not bad at all, actually."

He reached a tattooed arm to the top shelf. The guy had a tough, intimidating look about him, even though he was wearing a button-up with the sleeves rolled to his forearms, dress pants, and suspenders.

"Ah," he said with a grin. "Now you sound like a man who's ready to celebrate."

He poured a tumbler a third full and slid it across the bar top toward me.

Clasping the glass, I tipped it toward him. "Soon, my friend, soon. Right now, I'm just prepping for the hunt."

With a lift of his brow, he said, "A sportsman."

There was no missing the sarcasm behind it.

A smirk pulled at the edge of my mouth. "I guess you could say I'm a sportsman of sorts."

Amusement had him shaking his head, and he tapped the bar

top with the knuckles of one hand. "Just let me know if you need anything else."

"Will do."

He turned his attention to three women who'd sidled up to the bar, and I heaved a satisfied breath as I lifted the glass to my lips and took a sip. I was rolling it over my tongue, savoring the flavor, when a sound touched my ears.

It was laughter.

It was the kind of loud, messy laughter that typically would have annoyed the hell out of me. I had little patience for foolishness or nonsense.

Yet, there was something intriguing about it that snagged my attention, pulling at some place inside I didn't wholly recognize. There was absolutely nothing I could do but swivel on my stool, needing to see exactly from where and from whom it was coming.

Propping my elbows on the bar with the glass still clutched in my hand, I let my gaze hunt the room.

Landing on its mark.

It took a whole lot to stop me in my tracks.

Even more to impress me.

It wasn't that I was an asshole.

Okay, fine. Maybe it was exactly the fact that I was an asshole.

But I lived in New York City and had a place in Los Angeles. I traveled the world and wooed and entertained wherever I went. Half the time, women threw themselves at me in some kind of vain attempt to sweeten a deal.

Beautiful people were just a way of life.

So, how the fuck was it possible that the most gorgeous woman I'd ever seen was sitting across the room?

Her face was some kind of mesmerizing masterpiece. High, defined cheeks that tapered down to a narrow jaw and chin, sharp and distinct.

Unforgettable.

But her lips. Fuck, those lips.

They were red and full and delicious, so goddamned

15

appealing that I had the urge to walk across the room and demand a taste.

Her full attention was trained on the single woman sitting across from her, who was clearly goading her into debauchery.

The sex kitten of a woman pressed both her hands to the high-top table, as if she were searching for strength. Lush locks cascaded around her shoulders like a black river shimmering in the moonlight as she shook her head at whatever her friend had said.

My ear tuned in, keen and far too curious.

I didn't have time for distractions.

But here I was.

Distracted.

"I have work to do tomorrow," she said in a voice that struck me like a straight shot of lust. Low and deep and seductive. "You know I can't afford to mess this up. There's too much riding on it."

The other woman, who had short, messy brown hair, nudged a shot glass her direction. "Do it. I told you tonight was about unwinding. I'm not letting you leave here until you've forgotten all about the bullshit you're dealing with. Think of it this way…it will help you relax so you can get some good sleep tonight so you're ready and raring to go tomorrow."

A needy groan rumbled in my chest. I could think of a few better ways to leave her relaxed.

Satiated and satisfied.

All of them involved my tongue and my fingers and most definitely my cock.

The woman who was somehow making me lose a little bit of my head hesitated, working her lip with her teeth as she contemplated just how far she was going to allow herself to cut loose.

Then, as if she felt me staring at her, her gaze suddenly slanted my way.

I sucked in a stunned breath.

Vivid green eyes blinked back at me.

Emerald and ice.

Piercing.

Stunned.

As if she were just as affected by me.

Good God.

This woman.

I let my mouth tip up at the corner, relishing in the way those eyes went wide in surprise before they slid down my body. Just as quickly, she ducked her head and turned back to her friend, nodded, and tossed back the shot with a trembling hand.

Her pretty face pinched, that mouth puckering as she shook all over as she swallowed it.

I let loose a low chuckle, bringing my drink in for a sip as I pushed to my feet and headed in her direction.

I was a man who went after what I wanted.

And what I wanted right then was her. Even though she seemed resistant to look my way, I knew she felt it.

Knew she felt me.

That instinctual sixth sense that raised the hairs at the back of your neck and made your heart leap into action, thundering hard and low, your stomach quivering in awareness.

Run or freeze.

This girl?

She froze.

I came to a stop at the side of their table. "Is this seat taken?" I tossed out the most ridiculous cliché I could find as I gestured to the empty stool with my index finger of the hand still curled around my glass.

Another thing?

People loved clichés.

They really did.

It didn't matter how much they rolled their eyes and complained about it. They still flocked toward them. You know, that whole people don't like change mentality. It applied to all things.

The brown-haired pixie beamed up at me before she widened her eyes at the woman currently knotting my guts with a need unlike anything I'd felt in a long, long time.

"Why no," the pixie said as she waved a hand at the stool. "It just so happens it is not. I guess I was saving it for you. I'm Nikki."

I pulled out the stool and slipped onto the padded seat. "Ah, it seems a thank you is in order."

She angled her head. "This is the South. We're all about the hospitality." Her eyes made a pass over me. "You don't look like you're from around here."

I hefted a shoulder. "Just passing through."

I felt the movement to the right of me. The disturbance in the air as the woman who'd hooked me shifted in her seat. Her scent wrapped around me like ribbons, this rosy sweetness that made me itch to turn my head and bury my nose in her neck.

Inhale.

My gaze moved that way, a smirk already on my face when she tipped her chin so she was meeting my eye.

A tremble ripped down my spine.

Fuck.

One of the things that made me most successful? I could almost immediately get a read on people.

I instantly knew who was shady, keeping secrets and harboring ulterior motives, and who could be trusted, their cards laid on the table because they had everything to lose or everything to win.

Sitting a foot from me was a strong woman. Convicted. Fucking gorgeous, but I already knew that.

But the alcohol coursing her system had chipped away a few of the bricks that lined her defenses. Exposing a bit of something vulnerable in the depths of those emerald eyes that sparked as I met her gaze.

"Hi," I murmured, so low I was sure it was a growl.

I watched the thick bob of her throat.

Fear and attraction.

"Hi," she whispered.

"This is my Lily Pad, who was in dire need of a little fun," Nikki suddenly said as she leaned farther across the table.

I forced myself to look at her.

The girl admittedly was gorgeous, too, but in an entirely different way, not even close to being able to hold my attention the same way as this raven-haired beauty.

But with the way she was clearly trying to have a silent conversation with her friend, I knew she had as little interest in me as I did with her.

She was definitely playing fairy matchmaker for her friend.

With a flourish, she touched her chest. "And I am the Nikki Walters. We welcome you to Gingham Lakes. The bestest, smallest, coolest city in all the South."

"It's nice to meet you, Nikki."

I shot her a knowing wink before I slowly edged back to look at her friend.

The movement was weighted, igniting a crackle and a spark in the atmosphere.

Her lips parted.

"I'm Brody."

She seemed to hesitate before she finally let a smile ridge her perfect, delectable mouth.

God.

I wanted to eat her up.

"It's nice to meet you, Brody. I'm Lily…only that crazy thing over there"—she lifted her hand, palm out as she pushed it in her friend's direction—"gets away with calling me Lily Pad. And it seems she has me at a disadvantage tonight."

"Disadvantage?" I asked, playing it coy.

She rolled those fucking stunning eyes, and a tiny giggle slipped from her lips. "I'm not normally this loose."

The second she realized what she said, she slammed a hand over her mouth. "Oh my God," she cried against it. "I did not just say that." Her eyes squeezed tight as she shook her head.

Totally mortified.

And totally adorable.

Maybe that was the issue. The way she was dressed, she exuded power and strength, which I'd always thought of as the single quality required to get me hard.

But there was something soft about her, too. Something

intriguing and equally charming, this attribute that had me wanting to shift forward so I could get a better look.

"God…your shoulders…" She caught me off guard by blinking at me when she suddenly uttered the words.

"What?" I prodded, my voice deepening as I erased another inch of space between us.

"They're…" Her head barely shook as she struggled to find the words. "So big," she breathed.

A chuckle rumbled free as my brow arched. "You think it's my shoulders that are big."

She suddenly reached out, fingertips tracing my knuckles, sending a spiral of lust shooting through my veins.

"Like these hands?" she murmured with the shiver that took her whole.

I leaned forward, my mouth at her ear. "Among other things."

"I think that's my cue," Nikki suddenly said. Her stool skidded on the floor as she pushed it back, hopped to her feet, and grabbed her cocktail. "I'm actually over here getting hot and bothered watching the two of you." She waved her drink toward the same bartender who'd poured mine. "I'm going to flirt with Ollie over there and see if I can finally get that man to crack."

Lily giggled. Again. And again, I fucking liked it.

What the hell was wrong with me?

"Good luck with that," Lily said.

"With that man? God knows I'm going to need it," Nikki said before she spun and skipped toward the bar.

We both watched her go, saying nothing as a silence built in the space between us, growing thicker when I returned my hungry gaze back to her.

"So, Lily…tell me about you."

She wrapped both hands around her half-empty cocktail sitting in the midst of three empty shot glasses. She took a slow sip. "What would you like to know?"

"Everything." It was out before I could think better of it.

She shook her head. "Don't lie to me, Mr…"

"Brody," I instantly supplied.

"Brody," she settled on, as if maybe it too sounded as odd in her mouth as it did in mine. But there was something about sitting there that made me not want to be that guy who was here in her town to turn things upside down.

"Okay then, *Brody*, no lies. What do you really want to know about me?"

I reached out and wound a piece of her hair around my finger, moving in close, my nose just touching hers. "You really want the answer to this?"

"Yes." It was a wisp of a word that filled my senses.

Intoxicating.

"What I really want to know is if you taste as good as you look."

A soft gasp pulled into her lungs, and she edged back, watching me with those eyes. "Why do I get the feeling that, given the chance, you would swallow me whole?"

My mouth brushed the very corner of hers, the words a low promise where they grated from my tongue. "Believe me, baby, I might devour you, but you'll enjoy every second of it."

Her head rocked back a fraction, her lips parted, her breaths shallow. "I…" She blinked, as if she were searching for herself. "I…think I need to go."

"I think you should stay." She scooted back her stool and stood. She swayed as if she were struck with a wave of dizziness, her hands darting out to grip the table to keep her standing.

"Lily…why don't you let me take you home. I'll make sure you won't regret it."

She huffed a tiny laugh. "That's funny…because you have regret written all over you."

She leaned forward, and with a throaty murmur, her next words sank into me like a hook. "You stick around, Brody, come find me. Because I might be loose, but I'm not easy."

My mouth watered, and I gulped around the hunger, watching slack-jawed as she grabbed her red coat and purse and wound toward her friend at the bar.

She barely cast me a glance when they both headed for the door.

My fingers twitched.
The hunt was on.

four

Lillith

Drinks? **You are truly delusional, aren't you, Mr. Wolfe?**

I banged my fingers on the keyboard a little more aggressively than necessary before I directed the cursor to *send* and fired off the message with a nice, hard click.

Shots fired, asshole.

So maybe I shouldn't be returning messages at one in the morning when I was drunk and still a swoony mess over the gorgeous guy back at the bar.

Believe me, baby, I might devour you, but you'll enjoy every second of it.

Chills lifted as the memory of the man's words back at the bar skated across my skin like temptation and sex. My stomach twisted in a needy knot of want, desire rushing free as I thought of the magic that man would surely bring with his hands and that mouth and the *among other things*.

That sweet spot between my thighs sizzled and tingled.

I covered a giggle with my hand, and a hiccup followed it.

Okay.

I most definitely did not need to be messaging the asshole at one o'clock in the morning.

But I just couldn't help myself.

Not when I'd climbed into bed and pulled my laptop onto my lap after the relaxing night, so thankful that for a few moments I'd been able to shed the stress and the worry that had haunted me for the last five months.

Nikki was right.

I'd needed the break.

To unwind and let loose.

And God...oh God, had meeting Brody been exactly what the doctor prescribed. I'd known exactly where we were headed, and it had taken all I had to resist, to stand and force myself from the table.

A few flirty moments more, and the two of us would have been a tangle of limbs and needy hands.

Which in my book was nothing but a recipe for heartache and regret.

But that didn't mean I hadn't needed the attention. That I hadn't needed the bolstering. Someone to remind me I was beautiful and strong and appealing. Everyone needed encouragement before they set out for war.

So, I couldn't stop myself when I'd seen Wolfe had emailed me. With the audacity to ask me out for drinks, nonetheless.

I huffed and started to close down the lid when my inbox pinged.

"I bet you don't even need to sleep, do you, Mr. Wolfe. You aren't even human." It was all a mumble under my breath as I opened his message, hating the way my heart sped an extra notch.

Delusional? I think not, Ms. Redd. I'm merely giving you one last chance to come to your senses before you become an embarrassment. I am a gentleman, after all.

An embarrassment?

How dare he?

And a gentleman?

Hardly.

My fingers flew across the keys.

An embarrassment? Who me? I think you've forgotten who you're talking to. You are going to be the most embarrassed, embarrassed, embarrassed man to ever walk the earth. You just think you're so big and bad, don't you? Well guess what, I'm not afraid of you. Not at all. Because guess what? You're STUPID and arrogant and, just because you're supposed to be some gorgeous rich guy and everyone kisses your ass, it doesn't mean you always are going to get your way. The buck stops here, buddy. So, you can just turn around and go back from where you came, because you won't be blowing down any houses around here. Assholes like you are nothing but hot air.

I tacked on a nice, "Ha," when I hit send.

With a victorious grin, I quickly reread my words.

Dread curled in my stomach.

Oh God.

Shit.

No.

What did I do? What did I do?

Panicked, I looked around my bedroom as if I might find the message still floating in cyberspace. The only thing I wanted right then was the chance to put a stake in it.

Kill it dead.

I sounded like a blubbering fool.

I groaned in misery when my inbox pinged. Why did he still have to be awake?

Oh, Ms. Redd, I'm afraid it's you who is again confused. You seem to be lost in the wrong fairy tale. In the original story of Wolfe and Redd, I win. And did you just imply I'm gorgeous? Hmm...perhaps you do have a few things right, after all.

Grr. I wanted to scream.

Like I said. Arrogant.

Apparently, I just couldn't resist. I needed an intervention. But there I was, all by myself with no one to rein in the disaster I was galloping straight for.

Almost immediately, my inbox pinged.

I think you're confusing arrogance with confidence. I'll be packing plenty of it when I meet you tomorrow. And I promise you, at the end of it, I won't be the one who is embarrassed. Get your rest, Ms. Redd. You're going to need it.

I banged my head back on my pillow.

Shit. Shit. Shit.

What did I do?

"How do I look?"

I smoothed out my crisp, white blouse and straightened my pristine black pencil skirt that landed just below my knees. The uber professional outfit was set off with my hair up in an intricate but flowy twist so I could show off the emerald and diamond necklace I'd bought when I'd passed the bar.

It was my power piece.

It and the pair of super high black pumps that made me feel as if I held the keys to my own little kingdom.

That didn't mean I wasn't shaking in my boots.

"You look fabulous, as always," my assistant, Tina, said as she plucked a stray hair from my shoulder. "Nervous, though. You do look nervous."

I scowled at her. "Thanks for the vote of confidence."

"Hey, I didn't say you weren't going to slay this meeting. All I'm saying is you look a little nervous. You aren't even getting paid for this one. I don't get what the big deal is."

Maybe that was half the problem. No one really understood what the big deal was. Businesses came and went all the time.

"This is important to me," I told her.

"Obviously."

I glanced at my watch. "Two minutes."

"If he's as prompt as you."

I sucked in a steeling breath. "Something tells me he's every bit as prompt as I am."

"I'd better get out there then. Wouldn't want to keep the Big Bad Wolfe waiting, now would I?"

"Not helping," I told her.

"Just getting your blood pumpin'."

Exasperation widened my eyes, but Tina just grinned before she flounced from my office, leaving me with my nerves and the worry spinning through my mind.

Needing something to busy myself, I moved to where I had Addelaine's file opened on my desk. Nervously, I shifted through the papers while I was still standing, reciting the presentation and offer I'd memorized under my breath.

"You've got this," I whispered nearly silently right before my head jerked up when I heard the door click open.

My eyes went wide as my mouth dropped open, and I swore my damned heart came to a full stop, stuttered, and then tumbled before it took off at breakneck speed.

Anger bristled just under the surface of my skin as stunned disbelief shook my head.

In sauntered the most attractive man to ever take up my space. There wasn't any hesitation in his step when his head cocked to the side, and he sent me the most presumptuous, cheeky smirk as his eyes dragged over me from head to toe.

Arrogant.

Cocky.

Confident.

My hands trembled.

"You."

five

Broderick

You have to be shitting me.

A low rumble of disbelieving laughter filled my chest, and I bit it down, refusing to show Ms. Redd just how dumbfounded she had me. So maybe I stumbled a minor step at finding her standing in the office. Totally floored Ms. Redd and the fucking gorgeous woman who'd kept my dick hard all last night were one and the same.

Figured.

There had already been something about her that had me intrigued. Something that had me wired and excited at finally coming face to face with the woman who'd worked to cut me off at every turn, thwarting plans and throwing up roadblocks.

And somehow…I'd liked it.

It took my walking into her office for me to fully understand why.

"You…Brody…Broderick Wolfe," she sputtered through her own shock as that unmistakable attraction from last night lit up like the Las Vegas Strip between us, powered by the circuit of contention that had already been well-established.

I straightened my tie. "Ah, Ms. Redd, it's so very nice to see you again."

She heaved out an incredulous breath, her tiny hands fisted in little balls of indignation. "Did you...did you seek me out last night? Did you already know who I was? Were you following me?"

It was all a fiery demand that burned in all the right places.

God.

I liked this woman about just as much as I hated her.

I shot her a mocking smirk. "Who me?"

Her jaw tightened.

Damn, she was easy to rile.

Her attention fell to her desk, as if she were gathering herself, before she returned that emerald gaze to me, her chin lifted. "I'll have you arrested for stalking."

I almost laughed as I moved farther across the room. "Don't you think you're getting a little carried away, Ms. Redd? I find it presumptuous of you to assume it was me who searched for you to gain the upper hand. You were the one who knew I'd asked you for drinks. Perhaps you were the one stalking me."

Aghast, her pretty lips parted in a gust of fury, and her fists clenched tighter. "How dare you imply I would do anything outside of the law. I'll have you know, Mr. Wolfe, I take my position and all it entails very seriously."

"As do I."

"I doubt that." Her tone was a sarcastic blade.

My chuckle was low, laced with more amusement than it should have. "Then perhaps you should have done more homework, and you'd know full well how seriously I take my position and the ethical business policies and practices I demand."

A disbelieving huff jetted from between that goddamned, lust-inciting mouth that I wanted nothing more than to devour.

"You're going to stand there and pretend as if Wolfe Industries doesn't have a reputation for shady deals? Broderick Wolfe Sr. is infamous for infringements and wrongdoings. It's the platform on which your company was established."

The second she said it, anger rushed in to erase the lust, and the rigid, powerful exterior I always wore dropped for the barest moment as I grated the words. "This is my deal...not my father's, and I'd appreciate you not comparing me to him."

"It's all in the name, *Mr. Wolfe.*"

Rage bloomed in my blood, and I strode forward and pressed my hands to the top of the desk. I leaned over it in her direction just as she leaned mine. The two of us nose to nose. Breath to breath.

My heart hammered harder in the confines of my chest, and something more severe than the anger twisted through my nerves as I inhaled her sweet, rosy scent.

Her breaths became shallow, her eyes growing wide, and I swore I could smell her. Her need. Her want.

The need to consume her slicked across my skin like a slow, demanding burn.

"I. Am. Not. My. Father." It was a growl. He was the last thing I wanted her to see me as.

"No?" she challenged.

"No."

She lifted her chin, her face so close to mine my mouth was watering again. "Then prove it by not screwing over Mrs. Tindall."

My tone lowered. "Believe me, Ms. Redd, I will finalize this deal. And when I do, there will be absolutely nothing shady about it. I've been more than generous...more than fair to your client. It's you who is making unreasonable demands."

I leaned forward, my mouth at the tender lobe of her ear. "*Lily Pad.*" The last slipped from my tongue like a slow, promised threat.

Edging back a fraction, I reached out and ran my fingertip along the sharp, defined curve of her jaw, my eyes keen on the movement as I did. Her mouth dropped open just as I began to murmur deeply, "Mark my words...I will have that building, and then I will have you." I edged even closer. "Or maybe I'll have you first."

A shiver tumbled through her delicious body.

Blood still burning with an irresistible hunger, I forced myself away from her, adjusting the cuffs of my jacket as I tamped down the need that raged in my body, my dick hard and my determination at its height.

"What do you say we get started here, Ms. Redd? It seems we have work to do."

I rocked back in the chair where I sat in the office area of my penthouse suite that overlooked the twinkling lights that glittered and gleamed on the blackened waters of the river that ran through the middle of the city, fed by the two lakes at the base of the mountain that sat as a darkened silhouette on the near horizon.

Of course I was staying in the nicest hotel in the city which afforded an awe-inspiring view of the area.

That was at least until mine stood tall and proud in what would be the reclaimed city square.

Bigger and better than ever before.

Resolve settled into my bones, and I leaned forward to where I had my laptop sitting open at the end of the long conference table. I let my fingertips move across the keys.

Confidently.

Precisely.

Without question or hesitation.

Ms. Redd,

My offer is the best Ms. Tindall will receive. She can sell to me for more than double the value of the building, or I will simply bide my time until I can buy it from the bank once the property has been repossessed.

I'm not entirely sure what your end intentions are here, but it seems you're denying the inevitable, whether I'm involved in the equation or not.

But make no mistake. I am a part of this equation.

I never have been, nor will I ever be, a quitter, and I'm

more than eager to enlighten you on that fact. I've been told I'm a great teacher.

I always get what I want. *Always*. You'd do best not to forget it. Actually, I think there's little worry in you forgetting who I am. When I'm finished with you, the only thing you'll see when you close your eyes is *me*.

I pressed *send* while a thrill built up inside of me. God, I wanted that building if for no other reason than to prove to my father my approach was better than his. But I was beginning to wonder if I might want Ms. Redd more.

Six

Lillith

"Not a chance, Nikki. There is no way I'm going back to that bar."

Nikki spun around and started walking backward so she could face me as we strolled along the sidewalk. "And why on earth not?"

The newer buildings on Macaber Street towered on either side of us, and deep gray clouds grew with the threat of a storm where they glowed against the twilight.

That was exactly what I felt.

A storm coming.

Unsettled.

Unsure.

My brow lifted beneath my bangs. "Um…you do realize I basically told that bastard last night, if he wanted me, he would have to come hunt me down? If I show up there, he will actually think he has the chance of catching me. Ugh," I groaned. "I can't believe I didn't realize it was him. I mean…how many gorgeous strangers suddenly show up in Gingham Lakes? I must have sucker written all over my face."

She frowned at me. "He looked harmless, Lily Pad. Don't beat yourself up. There was no way you would have known. He was wearing jeans for crying out loud."

If it were possible, my brow lifted even higher.

She giggled. "Okay, he so didn't look harmless. He basically looked like he was ready to tear you to pieces in the best of ways. I think you're due for a little *shredding.*"

I swatted at her, my voice lowered so the elderly couple walking by wouldn't be subjected to our conversation. "Shredding? What is wrong with you? You're so disgusting. How are we even friends?" I muttered.

"Because you love me." She sang the words as she reached out and grabbed my forearm. "Come on, Lil-Lil. When's the last time you got laid?" It was almost a whine. Apparently my lack of sex life caused her physical pain.

"You know the answer to that."

So long ago I could barely remember. Or maybe it was because the sex was hardly memorable. Either way, it was completely pathetic.

She groaned as she spun back around, came to my side, and hooked her arm around mine. "See. That right there is a shame. Look at you. You're gorgeous and successful and probably the nicest, most genuine person I know, and you let UFF fuck up your mind and your heart. That is so not cool."

My eyes narrowed in confusion. "UFF?"

"Um…Unfortunate Fucker Frederick?" By her expression, I was sure she thought I'd lost my mind that I didn't know exactly what she was talking about.

"Unfortunate Fucker Frederick?"

She released an insufferable sigh. "Come on, Lily Pad. That dude didn't know up from down, if you know what I mean. Now, that shit is *unfortunate.*"

"Oh my God, why did I ever tell you that story?"

My skin crawled just thinking about my last boyfriend— Frederick. Gross. I'd broken up with his lying, cheating, stealing ass more than a year ago. I knew better than to trust the guy, or any guy, for that matter. I'd just gotten so….lonely. But lonely was a hundred times better than vulnerable and weak.

Nikki was right. The whole experience was *unfortunate*.

Luckily, I'd learned my lesson.

Nikki feigned a horrified gasp. "Because that's what best friends are for, which means you owe me all the stories. Plus, I warned you the second I saw that guy he was no good and up to no good, didn't I?"

"Yet, you're trying to drag me back to that bar?"

"Uh…yeah. You did see the man in question? Sometimes we luck out, and reality is even better than the rumors. And Broderick Wolfe is definitely all the rumors and more. Much, much more. And besides, that's *our* bar."

"He's the enemy."

"Who wants to do dirty, dirty things to you."

My stomach fluttered, and my heart beat faster. "You don't know that."

"Psh." She waved her free hand and steered us left so we cut across the street, rambling the whole way, "You know I have this sixth sense, and there are things I just know. And just like I knew Frederick would be all limpy and gimpy, I know Broderick or Brody or whatever you want to call him will blow your mind."

My belly lurched, thoughts of his promise from earlier today spinning through my mind, planting seeds of temptation I could never give in to.

"Even if he was the best lover on the face of the planet, you know there's no chance I'm letting that man touch me. He's trying to take Addelaine's building, for God's sake."

Even wanting him felt like a betrayal.

"What if he's not as bad as you think he is?"

"Oh, believe me, Nikki. Broderick Wolfe is the villain in this story."

She took another sharp right until we were standing in front of the very bar where I'd unwittingly met Mr. Wolfe last night.

She slanted me a wide, victorious grin. "Then maybe you need to show him exactly who the heroine is in this story."

Nervous energy skittered through my veins when I glanced at the signage above the bar. "He probably won't even be here."

God. Why did I feel disappointed at the thought?

Nikki pulled open the door. "There's only one way to find out."

He was there.

Of course, he was there.

Oh my God, he was there.

This was such a bad idea.

But there was no backing down when he swiveled in the stool and locked eyes with me.

A slow, predatory smile spread across his gorgeous face.

All teeth.

Tonight, he was wearing the same dark gray suit he'd worn to my office, but he'd lost the jacket and tie. The cuffs of his pink button-up were rolled to his elbows and the top two buttons were undone.

One ankle was hitched casually across his opposite knee, a tumbler full of amber liquid swishing in the crystal as he rocked back so casually in the stool.

But there was something so dominating in his blasé posture.

My knees weakened and my insides shook.

"Come on, let's get a drink," Nikki urged as she started toward the opposite end of the bar.

And there was absolutely nothing I could do but lift my chin as I started after her, my stride strong and purposed as I slowly untied the belt of my favorite red jacket.

He didn't even pretend as if he weren't watching me.

Didn't try to conceal the fact that he watched my every move.

Savored them.

Memorized them.

Hunting without moving an inch, his presence so big it was enough.

Because I already felt captured.

Entangled in his gaze.

"Ollie!" Nikki squealed.

God, the girl had it bad.

Ollie smiled his unreadable smile as he tossed two napkins down on the bar. The man was an enigma. Gorgeous in a tough, unattainable way. Quiet. Mysterious. And somehow, so utterly soft beneath the brute and tattoos and beard. "Your regulars? Or are you here to do it up big the way you did last night?"

A groan slipped free. "Don't ever let me drink that much again, Ollie, or I'm never coming back. My regular is perfect."

He chuckled. "Well, we can't have that now, can we?"

"Um, no, we definitely can't have that," Nikki added a bit too enthusiastically.

Ollie turned away and began making our drinks. I chanced peeking over at Mr. Wolfe, who'd swiveled a fraction so he was entirely facing my direction.

No shame.

He made a gesture, saying something silently to Ollie. Ollie returned whatever interaction they shared with a nod of his head.

Two minutes later, Ollie was passing Nikki her bright pink cosmo and me a glass of chardonnay. "Compliments of the gentleman at the end of the bar."

Oh no he didn't.

I scowled in Mr. Wolfe's direction, angling my head and pursing my lips as I pushed the stemmed glass away as if it were tainted. "No, thank you, Ollie. I'd prefer to pay for my own drink. If you'd return this to him."

Confusion passed through Ollie's expression before he shrugged. "Suit yourself."

He headed that way, passing the glass to Mr. Wolfe, who had never turned away and had witnessed the whole exchange. I shouldn't have been surprised when the arrogant man was already pushing to his feet the second he had the rejected wine glass in his hand.

Turning away, I tried to pretend I was in deep conversation with Nikki, searching for any subject to launch into. "Um...so it's supposed to rain, yeah?"

But it was no use.

There was no running.

A shiver flashed across my skin. Hot and cold as it raced and sped, tingling in all the places I couldn't afford to recognize this man. I tried to hold my breath, tried not to breathe in the faint scent of a spicy mandarin and sweet nutmeg.

His cologne dizzying.

Or maybe it was just him.

I felt the ominous presence eclipse me from behind. Because suddenly he was right there, his breath on my cheek and neck and ear. "I believe this belongs to you, Ms. Redd."

He reached around and set the glass down in front of me.

I struggled to rein in the mix of emotions that stampeded within me, this confusing dichotomy of hate and the crushing demand of my body.

Remember.

Remember why you're doing this.

Finding solid ground, I forced myself to look over my shoulder and meet his eye. "I can't be bought, Mr. Wolfe. I have no interest in you or your drink unless it will send you running out of town. So, why don't you go back to your seat, or more preferably, back to New York." The words grated from my tongue. God, this man brought out the worst in me. Made me crazy and angry and confused.

That penetrating gaze glinted and danced to a dark, dark beat, the hint of a smile twitching at his mouth.

He was laughing at me.

Of course he was.

"It's a drink, Ms. Redd. A peace offering. Not a goddamned bomb and certainly not a bribe. I was simply being nice."

Guilt tried to mix with the confusion he incited. I forced a dubious laugh. "Nice?"

He angled to the side and leaned his elbow on the bar so he could meet my eyes. He was so close he stole my breath. My sanity. "I could be...if that's what you wanted me to be. If you want, I'll promise not to bite." He angled closer, the words a low, guttural whisper. "But I'm pretty sure you want me to."

I jerked back, my breaths too shallow and my heart a wild thrum. I blinked through the daze. "You have a lot of nerve, Mr.

Wolfe, waltzing in here thinking you can just take anything you want."

A smirk climbed to his ridiculously gorgeous face. "Since when is it a bad thing to go after what you want?"

God, I had to get out of there before he mixed me up any more. I grabbed the glass he offered and tossed it back, draining the entire thing in one gulp before I slammed it back down.

If anything, the bastard looked satisfied.

My attention turned to Nikki, who was sitting there biting her lip as if she were watching some kind of ridiculous teen drama.

"I'm going to use the restroom and then head home," I told her.

Concern washed her features. "Are you sure?"

"I'm fine. I promise."

She hesitated, wary, before she nodded and waved her drink in the air. "I'm just going to finish this." There was no missing the longing in her voice, the undercurrent of why she was really there.

"I'll talk to you tomorrow."

I spun on my heels, took a single step, and then stalled, backing up to meet Mr. Wolfe's face, putting every ounce of strength I had into the warning. "The petition for historic landmark will be filed tomorrow. I will win this fight."

Then I strode away with as much poise as I could muster before I rounded into the hall and then nearly broke into a sprint when I knew I was out of eyeshot. I pushed open the restroom door, panting as I tried to regain my composure.

This was so not like me.

Needy and wanting things I could never have.

My willpower weak.

Why had I always gravitated to the people who would hurt me?

Addelaine had been the exception, which was why I couldn't let her down.

Finding my purpose, I moved to the sink, washed my hands, and dabbed a towel beneath my eyes as I studied myself in the mirror. My pupils dilated. My cheeks flushed.

God.

This was so stupid.

But that foolishness seemed to matter none when I swung open the door and stepped out into the darkened hall. Halfway down, my feet stopped short when I ran straight into the big body towering over me.

"Whoa, there, Lil' Redd." His words were as soft as silk.

A gasp rocked free, and my chest constricted, my thrumming heart going *whoosh, whoosh, whoosh* as I took a fumbled step back. He followed, angling around and backing me into the wall.

"Ms. Redd," he whispered, his glorious, ravaging face in shadows, those unmistakable eyes burning with fire and something deep. Something I couldn't quite recognize. He reached out and wound a lock of my hair around his big hand. "Lil' Redd. Who the fuck do you think you are?"

He inched closer, fingers fluttering along the edging of my coat, as if he were mesmerized by the color. It ignited the air in a furor of severity, his breaths mingling with mine, something alive. "Who do you think you are, driving me out of my damned mind? For months, I've been fantasizing about you, wondering why every time I opened one of your messages, my cock grew hard. Desperate for a taste of the unseen."

His mouth was at the shell of my ear, eliciting chills. "And now I know."

Oh God. What was he doing to me? And why did I like it so much?

"I can't do this," I mumbled, attempting to push him away. He captured my hands in his, brought them to his mouth, and kissed across the knuckles.

Shivers slipped down my spine, and oh my God, I was going to lose all control.

He leaned in closer, his mouth a whisper at my jaw. "You want me to chase you, Lil' Redd? *Run.*"

He suddenly stepped back, the expression on his face so severe I had the instinctual feeling that he needed me to run before he snapped.

I sucked in a shocked breath, turned on my heels, and

propelled myself forward and away.

Fled.

I ran out the door and into the night.

Rain poured from the raging heavens, streetlamps shone down through the haze. It created a kaleidoscope of light that glimmered all around me. I leaned over, sucking in breath after breath, knowing I needed to escape.

Run.

But I didn't get far.

Because he was suddenly there, his presence unmistakable where he appeared behind me.

Slowly, I turned around.

He stood there, looking like sin.

Drenched by the rain.

It only emphasized his beauty.

His strength.

I stood frozen while that attraction blazed between us. Zapping and demanding. Pulling and pulling and pulling.

I resisted all I could, the tension growing tight. It took all of five seconds before it was me who snapped.

I rushed his direction.

Hating the pull and loving it all the same.

I moaned when he twisted his hands in my soaked hair and spun me, pulling us into the alley before he had me against the wall and his mouth on mine.

Overpowering.

Overwhelming.

So fucking wrong.

So damned right.

His tongue licked out, tangling with mine.

His body hard.

Every. Inch.

"Oh God…you're so…big."

He rocked against me. "So much better to fuck you with."

I gripped his shirt. "There will be no fucking."

"No?" he challenged as he snaked a hand beneath my jacket and pushed my skirt up high enough that he was able to hitch my leg around his waist.

He angled me perfectly.

His hard cock against my lace-covered clit.

Pleasure pulsed. I gasped for a breath.

"Do you like that, Ms. Redd? Do you like the way you know I'm gonna feel?"

"Yes." It was a whimper when he rocked again.

His mouth moved along my throat, nipping at my chin, my lips. Nibbling and biting. I swore the man was eating me alive. The hand on my thigh roamed higher, scraping my skin.

His fingers slipped beneath the lace of my panties as the storm raged on around us. He edged back just as lightning flashed, his chiseled face vicious in the impact, dark, dark hair dripping across his forehead and his eyes...his eyes black with lust.

"I told you that when you closed your eyes I'd be the only thing you'd see." He drove three fingers inside of me.

A moan burst from my throat, and I rocked back against the hard brick wall. "Oh."

He fucked them in and out, his cock pressed into my thigh as a reminder of who he was, his fingers steadily driving me to a place I couldn't go.

His voice was grit as he uttered the words ferociously at my ear. "Your pussy is perfection. I can feel it, Lillith. How perfect it is. How tight and sweet. I can't wait until I make you mine. Mark my words. I will make you mine."

I wanted to fight and struggle and push him away.

Instead, my knees buckled when he rubbed his thumb in a demanding circle around my clit.

I clung to his shoulders, no longer able to stand.

His fingers drove deeper, his thumb magic as he circled and rubbed and coaxed.

Pleasure built.

Steadily.

Magnificently.

Destructively.

It split.

I swore I could feel the earth tremble around me as bliss rocketed through my being.

So good.

So good.

So good.

I couldn't see.

Couldn't think.

Couldn't stand.

I soared while I remained prisoner to the rain. Prisoner to the man.

Slowly, he eased his fingers out of me and took a step back while I stood there shaking. Shaking and shaking as I came down.

Way, way down where realization and ramifications set in.

Horror took hold of my spirit.

What did I do?

Oh my God, what did I do?

"You." It was a quiet, trembled accusation.

He sucked his fingers into his mouth. "I warned you to run. And you ran directly to me."

Before I could stop it, my hand cocked back, and I slapped him across the face. Then I turned and stormed through the driving rain.

I just couldn't tell if I was angrier with him or myself.

Seven

Broderick

A grin climbed to my face as I watched her as she strode out of the alley, the tail of that red coat whipping in the wind as freezing cold rain continued to beat down from above.

"That's right, Lil' Redd. Run. Because I'm really going to enjoy the chase," I murmured so quietly into the howling wind, forcing myself to remain standing as she raged down the sidewalk with her chin held high.

Hot waves of lust rippled through my muscles that strained with the effort of restraint. I wanted to chase her down. Push her a little further.

There was something about this woman that had me hanging on by a thread.

I wanted to get deep inside her.

I'd made that much clear.

But there was something more. Something dangerous about the way she forced me to slow down and listen. Take note. The intrigue and respect she commanded with the clear passion that burned through her spirit was never so clear than when we'd sat through the meeting this afternoon.

She'd stood there so sure and defiant, threatening to file the property with the National Register of Historic Places to stall our purchase of the building. Stating it was a historical landmark and citing all the reasons we should leave it standing.

As is.

Clearly, she was no fool, and she knew as well as I did there was little she could do to hinder or halt our plans. Instead, she'd appealed to our better natures with the thinly veiled promise of legal recourse.

She knew she had little grounds. Still, every word had been delivered with strength and an undercurrent of her base faith in humanity.

Somehow, it'd made me crave her all the more.

It was sheer strength that had forced me from her office.

Biding my time.

All too eager to show up at the bar this evening, knowing she would do the same, the lure too much for her to resist.

Shaking myself off, I turned the opposite direction and headed to my hotel, the luscious taste of her still on my tongue, my cock hard as stone as I rode the elevator to the top floor. Entering my suite, I went straight for my laptop still open on the conference table.

You are delicious. I knew you'd be. I can't wait for the full meal.

It took all of five seconds for a message to show in my inbox—just like I knew one would.

I'd rather starve.

I chuckled beneath my breath. God, there was nothing I liked more than a feisty woman. And I was beginning to think I liked this one best.

"Your father is pushing to close this deal by whatever means it needs to be done. So far, he hasn't sent anyone down there, but you know what will happen if he does."

Anger ratcheted up in my chest as I stared out the window from the backseat of the Lincoln, my attention hooked on the old building that had seen far better days. "I told him this was my deal and to stay out of it. I'm tired of him making a mess of things. There are protocols that need to be followed."

James sighed. "He's not exactly a man who listens to reason. What's the end goal here?"

I swallowed hard. "The same as it always is."

"Then I'll try to hold him off."

I nodded, even though I knew he couldn't see it. "Thank you for giving me the heads up."

"You know I always have your back."

"I do."

"Keep me posted."

"Okay," I said as I killed the call, giving myself a few moments to study my surroundings. Finally, I sucked in a breath, pushed open the door to the car, stood, and straightened my jacket as I headed straight for the door.

I didn't hesitate.

I just swung it open and strode inside as if I owned the place.

It was only a matter of time before I did.

My entrance didn't seem to faze the elderly woman who stood hunchback behind the counter. She just tilted her head a fraction to reveal her knowing, gray gaze.

Ah. No doubt, this was a woman who had seen many things. Made wise through the wounds of life.

"Addelaine Tindall," I said, my voice low but somehow soft.

She gave a slight nod. "Mr. Wolfe."

"I take it no introductions are necessary?"

A deep, short laugh echoed from her as she shook her head and went back to organizing the papers she had strewn across the counter. "That fancy suit you're wearing is really what gives it away. Considering I'm the only one in these parts who could make something so fine, I know you must be from out of town."

I began to wander the small storefront on the bottom floor, taking in the old pictures on the walls. The vast majority of them featured beaming brides in their custom wedding gowns. Others were family portraits that served as thank yous and endorsements. Proof of the talent that resided within these walls.

"Besides, men who look like you don't typically walk through that door, Mr. Wolfe."

I barely glanced back at her. "And what do I look like, Mrs. Tindall?"

"You look like a broken heart."

I hummed in question. "Do I really look that dangerous?"

The small sound she made was somehow both disbelieving and affectionate. Catching me off guard, it made me pause and shift so I could read her expression.

"Wasn't talking about you breakin' the hearts, young man. I was referring to your own."

I started to correct her ridiculous assumption but before I could, she winked.

A smile threatened, but I bit back my amusement. How was this woman making jokes when I was the one dragging her right up to the line?

I turned back to wandering the store, studying the pictures, my eyes going wide and my feet faltering when my sight landed on a cluster of pictures arranged on the wall near the counter.

Image after image of a raven-haired girl.

Young.

Beautiful then.

But different.

Broken.

Timid.

Not the bold woman who'd captured my thoughts and stoked my desire.

"She's something, isn't she?" Addelaine said from right behind me, startling me.

A lump suddenly felt prominent in my throat. I forced the heavy words around it. "I didn't realize she'd worked here."

Mrs. Tindall tsked. "Men like you often don't take the time to realize a lot of things. Look closer. You'll see she didn't just work here. She found herself here. I'd reckon this place was more like a home. A safe haven, if you will."

Realization settled into my bones. "Which is why she wants to save your store?"

She shrugged a thin shoulder. "Women like Lillith fight for what they believe is right. For what they believe is fair." She eyed me without fear. "So, why don't you tell me what you're doing here, Mr. Wolfe."

I fully turned around. "I came here to find out what it is you think is right."

eight

Lillith

I pounded on one side of the double doors. A frenzy of fury sped through my veins. It was the only thing that made me stupid enough to show up here. Of course he would be staying at the nicest hotel in town in the best suite. One call and I knew exactly where to find him.

I pounded harder.

Finally, the door to the penthouse suite flew open. My breath caught, and I swallowed around the awe that suddenly thickened my throat as a startling jolt of attraction flashed in the air.

God, how could I find this man so attractive?

He was so gorgeous. So appealing and big and bad.

I hated him, didn't I?

I took a deep breath and found my resolve. Yes, I hated every single perfectly sculpted inch of him. I fisted the reason for my hate in my hand and charged passed him through the door. I spun around and shoved the paperwork his direction. "What is this?"

He widened his eyes as he let the door fall closed. "Please, Ms. Redd, *do* come inside."

"I asked you what this is." My voice was gravel as my gaze flashed down his body.

Desire burning me from the inside out.

I tried to stop them, I did, but I was assaulted by the memories of the alleyway from last night

His fingers.

His mouth.

Heat swept across my flesh.

I looked away, as if I were suddenly interested in taking in the luxury of his suite. The area was dim, only a spray of light that tumbled in from the attached bedroom to my right cut across the floor. A living area was at the front and a long conference table was set up in the back near the floor-to-ceiling windows. It offered an awe-inspiring view of the city I loved.

The reason for my visit.

I turned my attention back to him and refused myself the pleasure of taking in his glorious face or his irresistible body. It was close to impossible to do, considering his shirt was unbuttoned, showing off a hint of the toned, olive skin of his chest and abdomen.

Oh God. This was so very bad.

I struggled to keep my mouth from trembling when I spat the words again. "What is this?"

He looked at me as if he couldn't believe I could be so dense. "A contract of sale."

"I know it's a contract of sale. What I want to know is how you already have it and why Addelaine Tindall signed it."

He stood a mere ten feet from me, the lines of his face playing in the shadows.

He slowly stalked forward. "I warned you, I always get what I want."

"Not this time, you don't. I told you I would see to it that building remained intact. I know her signature was coerced, and I intend to prove it."

In a flash, he was in my face, his stance fierce and bristling as he backed me deeper into the space. "I would suggest you get your facts straight before you barge in here making accusations."

My teeth grated. "She would never sign this of her own free will. I *know* her."

He pried my fingers from the papers I fisted and tossed them onto the table I hadn't even realized he had me backed against. "Ms. Redd, maybe you think you have it all figured out, or maybe you know absolutely nothing at all."

"I know you're an asshole." It was a whisper against his lips. His lips that were suddenly crushing mine.

It was a tyranny. The way his mouth moved over mine and his hand fisted in my hair, jerking my head back as he commanded the kiss.

Aggressively.

Precisely.

Air shot from my lungs when he hoisted me onto the table, a massive hand gliding up my backside as he pushed up my skirt. He greedily gripped my ass. "I bet this ass will feel just as good as that sweet cunt."

"Fuck you." I hissed the words as I tore his shirt free from the wide, foreboding strength of his shoulders, exposing the raw beauty of this overpowering man.

Desire spiraled, pulsed, and ached.

He wedged his hips between my thighs as the demand of his kiss intensified.

Devouring.

Provoking.

His hands were at the belt of my jacket, tugging at the loop, setting it free. "Red drives me wild. Did you know that, Lillith? Did you know finding you standing in my doorway in it was nothing less than a provocation. A bull set to charge."

"I hate you," I barely managed.

"Are you sure about that?" he crooned. "Maybe you're wrong about all of that, too. I think you want me just as badly as I want you."

A moan rolled from my tongue when he yanked my coat down my arms and peeled it from my body. The movement forced me back. His mouth was instantly on my neck, licking and biting, building a frenzy of need in my belly.

My fingernails dug into his shoulders as he rocked against my center.

Need lit up like a torch behind my eyes, and my full focus turned to the button and zipper of his pants, tugging them loose.

"What am I doing?" It was all a delirious jumble of words as he gripped my breasts in both of his enormous hands before sliding them against my belly and rushing them up beneath the satiny material of my blouse, stoking flames across my skin.

He tore the fabric over my head.

"You're getting ready to find out just what it's like to have a man you'll never forget."

He released the clasp of my bra. The cool air that blew across my nipples beaded them into tight, hard peaks. He leaned down, flattened his tongue across one in the same second he was twisting out of his pants and his underwear.

My fingers drove into his hair. Tiny sparks of pleasure shocked through my body. Tightening my belly and throbbing between my thighs. Teeth scraped my chin. My neck. "Asshole," I whimpered.

"Bitch," he grated before my skirt and underwear were gone, casualties of this man who laid every reservation to waste with every hungry touch.

God, how badly I needed this.

And how badly I hated I did.

I gulped when I realized we both were bare, my eyes wide as I took him in where he towered over me.

Everything about him was compelling.

Formidable.

Unstoppable.

Irresistible.

Every sculpted inch of his body was perfection.

But his eyes…his dark, dark eyes were demanding something I couldn't read.

"You won't win this," I somehow managed as I stared up at him, my chin rigid.

He gripped it between his thumb and forefinger, his words a breath against my lips. "I already have."

That was right in the same second a frenzy of movement ignited between us. The man covered his cock with a condom in the flash of a second before he fisted himself at the base, his dick just parting my slit.

My head spun, dizzy with desire and a hint of pain as he spread me.

"Oh…oh…" I panted for coherency. "You're…too big."

He gripped my thigh, and his teeth clenched as he worked himself inside. "Big is better, baby. I thought we already established that."

"I'm more a 'how you use it' kind of girl." Where that came from, I had no idea. But with him, I couldn't stop. The hostility that raged against this attraction I didn't understand. An attraction too great. Something beyond reason.

Because this was insanity.

He gripped my knees, spreading me wide. Wider and wider. My hands barely clung to the edge of the table as he rocked, thrusting deeper with each pass. Deeper and deeper.

The clutch of my walls taking him. Needing him.

He groaned a guttural sound when he finally seated himself fully. It was something animalistic. Primal. "I knew it. I knew your pussy would be perfection. Sheer, utter perfection."

His fucks grew harder, a demanding concoction that escalated with each deadly stroke. His hands slid from my knees to under the inside of my thighs, lifting me so he could get a better angle.

"Tight and sweet. I told you I'd make you mine. I told you. You're mine, Lil' Redd. Fucking mine."

His fingertips evoked some kind of madness where he ran them along the crease of where we were joined, brushing all the way back to the pucker of my ass, before his thumb came insistent against my clit.

My head flailed as I fought the mounting pleasure. My nails raked across his magnificent chest and down his stomach.

"Stop fighting it. Stop fighting me. Trust me," he growled.

"I don't trust you at all." I raged against the drive of his body that nearly sent me over the edge with each deep, decadent stroke.

A buzz bloomed in the deepest well of my body.

Physical.

Spiritual.

I no longer knew.

Building and building. Tingles shimmered and danced. Growing in intensity.

"Trust me," he demanded as he pressed down on the base of my belly with a palm, his thumb magic where it stroked me into bliss.

Shattering, all-consuming bliss. A torrent that flowed and lifted and spun.

I cried out, gripping his shoulders as he thrust harder and faster and deeper until he roared, his teeth flashing in the night before they sank into the flesh of my shoulder.

It sent another shot of pleasure to my clit.

Aftershocks.

Quake after quake.

My foundation shattered.

He threaded his fingers in my hair, panting at my cheek. "Trust me. I promise you I won't hurt her."

nine

Lillith

Throat dry, I gaped out my doorway in shock at the man standing there, not sure if I wanted to slam the door shut or go running through it.

"What are you doing here?" I managed with a pull of my brow, my thoughts just catching up to my heart that was racing ahead of me. "How did you even know where I live?"

Broderick tsked. "Come now, Ms. Redd. It's a small city where the dirt doesn't run all that deep. It took nothing more than asking about you at the restaurant in my hotel to gain that information. And don't tell me you weren't missing me." He was dressed in worn jeans and a casual button-up like he had been the first night I'd met him. Only this time, the morning light cast him in a kind of warmth I didn't think I'd ever associated with him before, his eyes softer than they'd ever been.

That didn't mean there wasn't a smirk twitching at the corner of his gorgeous mouth, something powerful and threatening beneath the informal disguise.

Heat flashed across my skin as my thoughts roared back to last night, and I sucked my bottom lip between my teeth as I looked at the ground for a beat while I gathered my courage and thoughts.

I still couldn't believe what I'd done. How I'd let myself go. And how much I'd liked it.

I forced myself to look back at him. "So, now you really are stalking me. And does the fact you showed up here mean you were missing me?"

Now I was teasing him.

I'd lost all control.

A grin danced across his full lips. "Maybe."

He took a step forward, his voice suddenly a low rumble that shivered across my skin. "You were quite unforgettable last night. I have to admit that after you left, my bed had never felt so cold."

"You don't need to play me. You already got what you wanted."

He wound a finger in my hair, his head cocked to the side, those dark eyes ablaze. "That's where you're wrong. I've only started."

I swallowed around the attraction, trying to find footing beneath his striking severity.

He stepped back, giving me space. "Come with me. I want to show you something."

Hesitation warred with the want that tumbled through my belly. "I have work to do. I need to get to the office."

"I think this will be well worth your time."

Doubt hovered in the air between us before he reached out and tugged at my hand as he took another step backward. "Come on, Lil' Redd. There's no need to be afraid."

A scowl climbed to my brow, though somehow a tease slid out with the words. "Really...I think I already bear the proof that you bite."

He laughed. Straight belly laughed. Confusion twisted through my spirit, an inkling of something I didn't quite understand—something sweet and hopeful—before he tugged me closer, his mouth at my temple. "Do you know how much I like you, Lily Pad?"

I blinked into his shirt, wondering how it was possible that I was starting to like him, too. "You don't even know me."

"Oh, I think I know you well enough, don't you?" He pulled back to shoot me a wink before he was threading his fingers through mine and leading me to the car parked at the curb in front of my house. "Come."

And I had no idea if it was distrust or excitement that flapped in my belly when I let him lead me to his car.

Ten minutes later, Broderick made a left in his rented Audi. The realization of where we were going injected a dose of anxiety into my system, and I leaned forward in my seat, my voice riddled with doubt. "Why are you bringing me here?"

My gaze traveled the line of old buildings that sat like a beacon. A harbor. My safe haven.

He slowed when he came to the shabby three-story building that housed Tindall's Thimbles. Easing up next to the curb, he put the car in park but left the engine idling.

He shifted in his seat to face me. "Because I want you to understand my goals. My vision. I want you to know why Addelaine Tindall signed those papers."

Unease stirred through my senses. Along with a shot of hope. I met his gaze. Fully and without restraint. "Tell me."

I watched the thick bob of his throat, his voice hoarse. "I am not the bad guy, Lillith. Evil might run through my veins, my blood my father's, but I have fought his brand of corrupt morals my entire life. I'm not here to ruin people's lives. I'm here to make them better. And if stamping my father's name on a project makes me the bad guy, too, then so be it. I love winning, Lillith. I won't lie. But my wins are on my own merit, and they are always, always fair."

I shook my head. I wanted to believe him, but all my reservations warned me to remember exactly who I was dealing with. "But you pushed this purchase without concern for Mrs. Tindall. Just like the rest of the buildings your company acquired."

A scowl marred his face. "How could you say without concern? Every financial offer I've made has far surpassed the current value of any of these holdings."

Frustration bubbled inside of me. "But that's it, right there. There is no dollar value that can compensate for memories. For heritage."

His gaze slid to the plate glass of Addelaine's store. "Is that what you're trying to protect, Lillith? Your memories? Is all of this about you?"

Somehow, the words that fell from his mouth were as soft as they were sharp.

As if there was a chance he might understand and he was accusing me of an agenda at the same time.

Old wounds flared. I attempted to stuff them down where they belonged. Apparently, I didn't succeed because my voice cracked as I pressed my palm over my heart. "I'm fighting for the woman who gave me everything. I'm fighting for her legacy. I'm fighting for her family and her friends and all the people who have stories like hers."

His arm suddenly shot out, his hand fisting in my hair, his tone emphatic. "What if financial compensation is the only thing I have to offer them? What if it's the only thing I can do to save what they've created? The only way I can help preserve what they've made of themselves?"

My heart thrummed in the confines of my chest, my eyes darting across his face, desperate to read the truth in his expression. "What are you saying?"

He grimaced. "I'm saying my father has already made his decision. This street will bear the Wolfe name. Our hotel will stand here, in this spot, one way or another. His way or my way. And I promise you, my way is best."

Awareness settled over me, like a rock sinking to the pit of my stomach.

His thumb brushed over my cheek. "Addelaine signed that contract because when I went to see her, I asked her what *she* wanted. I asked her what she believed was fair in this situation. She felt the purchase offer was more than fair, and additionally, she asked for six months to find a new location before the sale closed. I agreed, and she signed. She and I? We made a deal.

There was no coercion."

Regret twisted through my consciousness.

Had I pegged him wrong all along?

"Then why isn't that six month promise in the contract?"

"Because my father is pushing for a closed deal. I give that to him, and he moves on to his next acquisition. It's an easy distraction."

I wanted to believe it. In him.

A wry grin pulled at his mouth as his gaze traveled to the storefront. "She's an incredible woman. Smart. But she's also flexible." He moved his other hand to my face, framing both sides when he looked back at me. "And that's what I'm asking you to be. Flexible."

There was no missing the innuendo behind it.

God, he had me tied up in knots. Because there I was with butterflies in my stomach and a blush on my face. The man made me vulnerable in a way I hadn't allowed myself to be in so many years.

Broderick Wolfe brought out the best and the worst in me.

"What do you want from me?" I finally whispered.

His hands tightened. "First…I want you to say you trust me and to drop that silly application to make the building a historic monument. You and I both know it won't stick."

Fire glinted in his dark, dark gaze. "Then, I want to take you back to my suite so I can fuck you again, and then from there, you and I can see where this goes."

"Where this goes?" It came off as incredulous.

"Yeah, Ms. Redd. We'll see where it goes. I loved the taste I got last night. Something tells me I won't ever get enough."

My spirit lurched. Reaching toward something that should be impossible. Because I was supposed to hate him.

He smiled that magnetic smile.

And I realized that was what terrified me the most about him. I didn't hate him at all.

"And you'll give Mrs. Tindall six months?"

"Six months."

"Promise me this isn't some kind of trick." A plea slipped

into my tone because I'd opened myself to him in a way that gave him the complete upper hand, every advantage in his corner.

God, the last thing I needed was to be lured into a trap by this mesmerizing man. Let my guard down so he could rush in for the kill.

"Trust me," he said again.

"I'm not sure I know how."

"Then let me prove to you that you can." His fingertips trailed down the hollow of my throat, a dark promise coating the words, "Do you trust me with this body?"

"Yes." A shiver raced down my spine, settling low, igniting a throb between my thighs.

Broderick sat back, that arrogance setting like stone on every line of his magnificent face. "Good. Then let's find out where this goes."

ten

Broderick

"Do you trust me?" I whispered close to her ear where she was bent over the side of my bed, her hands pressed to the mattress.

Shivering, she nodded, locks of raven hair cascading around her shoulders. Her back was bare and just as gorgeous as the rest of her, and I slowly trailed my fingertips down the length of her spine, all the way down to the only thing she wore.

A red, lacy thong.

That and a pair of red high, high heels.

Lust tightened my balls and hardened my dick.

Yes.

"I love red," I murmured as I dipped my fingertips between her cheeks and glided them over the fabric. "So fucking much."

She whined, her ass jutting out, asking for more.

"Did you wear these for me?" The question rumbled from deep in my throat. "Did you know I would come for you? Find you? Take you?"

A whimper slipped from her mouth.

"Tell me," I demanded.

"Yes." It was a breath. "Please."

Hunger ricocheted through my body.

Something primal.

Fueling the obsession she'd incited in me since the first time my eyes had scanned across her impassioned words.

But standing there, a different kind of emotion rushed me. Something bigger. Something more.

I swallowed around it as I dropped to my knees behind her, forcing her legs apart and situating myself between them. My palms cupped her cheeks, spreading her. "Your ass is as perfect as your pussy, Lillith. Did you know that? Did you know every inch of you drives me wild?"

I pressed my nose to the fabric of her underwear, which did nothing to cover her, and inhaled deeply. "You smell delicious."

No. Not like flowers or sugar or chocolate.

She smelled like a woman. She smelled like sex. She smelled like *me*.

A growl pulled from my lungs, and I licked the wet, glistening flesh that peeked out from the fabric before I nudged the lace aside so I could go deeper. Fucking my tongue into her tight heat and running my fingers along the crease of her ass.

She moaned. "Broderick."

I bit the inside of her thigh.

She yelped.

"I'm going to devour you, Lillith. Every inch."

Her legs shook. "Yes," she whispered.

I edged back a fraction so I could pull her thong from her waist and drag it down her legs, sitting back on my heels so I could appreciate the view as I unwound them from her feet.

The lights were off in my room, and only sheer drapes shaded the windows from the winter day.

It cast her as a silhouette.

Sleek and sexy.

"You are so damned beautiful," I murmured when I gripped her by the outside of the legs. I edged forward, tongue gliding into her folds.

"Brody." Her saying my name that way had me close to coming unhinged, and I angled so I could lave attention on her clit. I flicked and circled while she writhed and moaned. "Please...more...don't stop."

My hands explored. Greedily. Skating her soft skin, her legs, her round bottom, and the small of her back.

God, she was a miracle.

Appealing in a way that had hit me like a flash flood. Unaware and unprepared.

I swept my fingertips through the desire that coated her, teasing before I plunged them inside.

"Like this?" I demanded.

I drove them deep, making her jerk with the sudden pleasure.

"Yes," she begged then cried out in frustration when I pulled them free before she was squirming and panting and flailing again when I brushed them up the sensitive flesh at the back of her pussy and to the tight pucker of her ass.

"Trust me," I whispered against her skin, kissing along her inner thigh as I continued to touch her. Tease her. Taunt her. "Tell me you trust me."

She warred, her words a wisp of concession. "I...I trust you."

I had to suck in a breath to steady myself.

Because I could feel something wanting to give.

Something rigid and hard wanting to go soft.

She whimpered and gave, her legs shaking as she struggled to relax as I slowly eased two fingers inside. "You're mine, Ms. Redd. Do you hear me? I told you I'd make you mine."

Her low moan echoed from the walls as I slowly drove my fingers deeper, her knees weakening as she clawed at the bed.

"I...I can't...please."

"Please what?"

"I need you," she pleaded.

Swiftly I stood and pulled my fingers free before I sank the fingers of both hands into her ass cheeks, my cock catching on her pussy as I nudged in an inch. "Is this what you need?"

Desire blazed.

"Yes. Please...don't tease me. I'm yours."

I'm yours.

I was consumed by the confession of her words, and I drove

my cock deep inside her body. Her walls spasmed with the intrusion, clutching my dick in needy desperation.

"Fuck…you feel amazing, Ms. Redd. So fucking good. Tell me how good my cock feels. This is why you won't ever get away from me."

The words spilled out without thought or reason.

The only thing I knew was their truth.

I would never let this woman get away from me.

I would hunt her. Find her. Keep her.

"I…oh my…fuck." It was all an incoherent jumble of words from her gorgeous mouth as she struggled to keep standing as I began to fuck her—hard and fast.

Unbridled.

Wild.

Claiming.

Her flesh stretched around me, gripping me in its satiny welcome.

Offering it all.

So, I took it.

With each fierce thrust, she cried out, her fingers digging into the comforter of the bed. I ran my thumb around her slickness, gathering it as I dragged it upward and pushing it into her hole. My other fingers wound around to her front, grabbing her tit, her throat, before I forced two fingers into her mouth.

She sucked me with her hot, wet tongue while her hot, wet body clutched and begged and moaned.

Completely unhinged.

As unhinged as I was.

My head spun and her body bowed and I was suddenly overcome.

Staggered in a way I wasn't sure I could afford to be.

A surprise gasp flew from her when I pulled out, picked her up, and tossed her onto her back on the bed.

And there she was. All spread out, raven hair and milky skin and red high heels.

I was quick to crawl over her, caging her for a heated moment, staring down at her gorgeous face as I felt something shatter inside me.

I drove back into her, pleasure spiking as I filled her.

And she watched me with those emerald eyes. Her lips parted. Her heart clear.

"Redd," I whispered, "what have you done to me?"

"It's you who's taken me." Her words were a wispy admission.

I edged back so I could run my knuckle over her clit.

That single touch was all it took.

She arched from the bed as she slammed into ecstasy. Her head rocked back and those perfect tits jutted toward my face.

My mouth grazed a rosy nipple as I eased my hand away before both my hands were on either side of her head as I conquered her with each erratic thrust.

Pleasure rushed down my spine. Tightening my balls. Constricting to a pinpoint.

Exploding and blowing through my body on a fiery circuit.

Every nerve.

Every cell.

I poured into her, my body bowing and my head dipping down to the soft flesh of her shoulder.

My teeth sank in.

Making my mark.

Sated, I collapsed onto her sweat-drenched body before I pushed up onto my elbow and brushed my fingers through her hair. "I think I like where this is going."

Lillith giggled. "I think I do, too."

She sobered, touched my face, vulnerability slipping into her tone. "I shouldn't fall for you."

I edged down and nipped at her bottom lip. "Yes, you should."

eleven

Lillith

"That was amazing," the deep voice grumbled from beside me, his rugged pants rising into the air as night took hold of the hotel room.

I struggled to find my own breath. My body blissfully spent.

But it was my heart pulsing full of an overwhelming satisfaction and joy that shivered through my senses. The feelings pressed and pulsed and thrummed, demanding to make themselves known.

Affection.

Fondness.

Care.

Stripped of my anger, they were right there, taunting me with the fact I'd rather be in his arms than anywhere else.

I knew those feelings put me in greater danger with this man than I'd ever been.

I rolled onto my side and propped up on my elbow. "What is happening here?" I whispered.

Broderick lay on his back in the middle of the massive bed we'd spent the entire day utilizing to its fullest potential.

I couldn't resist tracing a fingertip down the sheer strength of his bare chest and over his ripped abdomen. As if I hadn't spent the last eight hours exploring every inch of him while he'd consumed every inch of me.

No place in me had been left unattended. He'd taken me hard and fast and rough, again and again. Until the last time when his touch had turned tender and slow as he'd stared down at me through the descending night.

He grinned. "I thought we were seeing where this goes."

"But now that you have things settled here, you'll be going back to New York."

"Will I be?"

Quickly, I shifted up farther so I could get a better look at him. "What?"

He raised a hand and threaded his fingers through my hair. "Maybe you were entirely wrong about my view back in Manhattan, Lillith. Maybe I have the best view right here."

Tingles spread like sparking matches to my spirit.

Stunned, I blinked down at him. "You want to stay here…because of me?" It almost came across as an accusation.

"You think I wouldn't?"

My head shook. "You don't even know me."

His smile was easy. "You keep saying that."

He seemed completely unperturbed by my sudden questioning, while my whole world felt as if it'd spun off its axis.

I was a realist.

A planner.

Cautious to the ninth degree.

I didn't carelessly fall in love. To me, love was a decision that was made only by choice, given after every consequence had been taken into consideration.

Otherwise, you were left stung. Bitten. Broken.

I also didn't fall recklessly into someone's bed.

Yet, there I was.

"I keep saying that because it's true."

"What are you so afraid of?" he asked as he ran gentle fingers through my hair, a frown denting between his eyes.

I had the sudden urge to slip from his bed and cover myself, hide, the impulse stronger than it'd been in a long, long time.

His brow furrowed, the man so intent as he ran the knuckles of one hand down my cheek and under my jaw. Tingles lifted. Warmth and comfort and a stroke of that fire. "Who hurt you, Lillith?"

"The people who were supposed to love me most."

I had no idea what had come over me, because the urge to tell him was suddenly so much greater than the need to run. The pain I'd kept hidden for so long begging to be released. He watched me, silently coaxing me to continue.

I swallowed around the lump in my throat before I forced out the confession. "I was fifteen…"

I blinked through the memory, my voice going soft as I got lost in it. "It was just like any other day. I went to school. My momma had been more scattered …flustered. Depressed maybe, I don't know."

My tongue felt as if it might freeze up, but the words kept flooding out when Broderick tightened his hold in my hair. "I let myself into the house after school that day, and they just…were gone. She and her boyfriend. I kept calling for her, thinking it was some kind of joke. I ran to her room and all the drawers were open. Empty. She'd left me this letter…telling me she was sorry and that everything would be okay. That I was a *big girl*."

Something that looked like anger took hold of his expression before awareness settled into its place. Slowly, he nodded in understanding. "And Addelaine took you in."

"Yeah. I answered a call for a help wanted ad, naïve enough to think I'd make enough money to keep paying rent on the house. But Addelaine and that store…they became my home. I lived with her until I graduated from college."

He smiled. "I knew she was an amazing woman."

"She is."

"Like you," he murmured, brushing his lips across mine.

Butterflies tumbled. My heart full. The rigid pieces splintering beneath the weight of his care. And suddenly I was wanting things I hadn't dreamed of wanting in so long. Maybe Nikki was right. I needed a little shredding. But it was my distrust and skepticism that this man was shaving away.

Silence hovered in the air. "I should probably go."

"Oh no, Ms. Redd. You aren't going anywhere."

My brows lifted as my mouth pulled into a smile. "Is that so?"

He grinned. "I thought we already established you don't need to be afraid."

My fingertips raked across the strength of his chest, and I peeked up at him. "But I am. I'm afraid of this. It's insane that I'm here. You're the last person I should fall for."

His big hand cupped the side of my face. "Don't you know all great love stories never should have been? That's what makes them great."

"Is that what you think this is…the start to a great love story?"

"Do you want it to be?" There was a tease behind his words, but a softness, too.

Heat flashed across my skin, warming me inside and out. "That's…crazy. Just last night, I hated you."

But there I was, smiling down at him like a lovestruck fool while I said it with something powerful and wonderful threatening to burst, the weight inside of me so much lighter since I'd admitted to him the root of so many of my fears.

A low chuckle rumbled from his chest. "You didn't hate me, Lillith. You were afraid of me because I made you feel things you didn't want to let yourself feel. You wanted me, and you hated that I had that effect on you."

His hand cinched down tighter. He yanked my face down close to his. "You hated that you couldn't say no."

It was a tease.

It was the truth.

That attraction flashed.

A wildfire.

Broderick guided me over him, his cock already hard as he aligned himself with me. "I told you that I always get what I want. And what I want is you, and that's not ever going to change."

What I couldn't comprehend was how this man who'd been my enemy for five months had made me want him in less than three days.

Because there was nothing I could do when I slid down onto his length but give him all of me.

My body. My heart. My trust.

Disoriented, I blinked into the shadows of the darkened room. Slowly, I came to awareness. Broderick's big, warm body was next to mine where he was lost in the contentment of sleep, his breaths deep and slow.

I sank back into the comfort of him, nestling closer as I let my eyes drift closed. Seconds later, they popped back open when I realized what had originally pulled me from sleep.

His phone lit up on the nightstand on his side of the bed and vibrated against the glass.

Telling myself to ignore it, I forced myself to close my eyes and go back to sleep, only for the offending noise to recur.

Leave it, I silently told myself. But I couldn't escape the tingle of worry that buzzed at the back of my brain.

Apprehension twisted through my nerves. Prodding and pinching and warning.

I sucked in a breath, trying to convince myself I was only this way because this relationship was new and it'd started on bad terms. I'd just come to recognize the side of the man that was good and honest.

We'd been a whirlwind.

Caught up. Shot to the highest high before I'd even realized I'd been swept off my feet.

That was why I felt unsettled.

It had to be.

I heard the vibration of his phone again.

Would it be so wrong to peek? Maybe it was an emergency. It was the middle of the night, after all.

I sat up, holding a decadent sheet to my bare chest, feeling like such an asshole for doing this but unable to stop as I peered through the darkness to the nightstand. I hesitated and then finally gave in.

I reached over him and glided a shaking finger over the screen to find the series of texts that screamed back from Broderick's phone.

All of them from Rex Gunner, the owner of the most successful construction company in Gingham Lakes. A man I knew well. A man I trusted and admired.

A heavy lump grew in my throat as I skimmed through his words.

If you think I'm going to bulldoze those buildings two weeks from tomorrow, you are insane.

Do you think I don't know it's impossible to get permits that quickly? Someone got paid off to make that happen.

I told you I work on the up and up.

Gut told me something was off the second you walked into my office.

Deal is off.

Dread slicked my skin in a hot sheen of sweat and nausea rolled in my stomach.

I pressed my hand to my chest to try to stop the ache blossoming there as tears sprang to my eyes.

I should have known. I should have known.

You fool. You stupid fool. He played you. He played you just like they all do.

Knees weak, I slipped off the bed, trying to stand. Moisture blurred by sight as I fumbled with my clothing, trying to be as quiet as possible as I slipped out of the bedroom and into the main area of the suite.

I dressed in the dark, piecing my exterior back together while everything inside shattered.

I grabbed my purse from where I'd left it on the entryway table, fumbled with the knob, and slipped out into the hall. My breaths were shallow, my mind racing with how I could possibly fix this. Panic took hold of my spirit, and my feet moved faster and faster as I made my way down the hall and to the elevator.

I didn't even have my car.

But I didn't care.

I would do whatever it took to fix my mistake.

I jerked to a stop in front of the modest house on the outskirts of town. A light blazed from the porch, Rex Gunner visible through the sheer curtains as he ambled around his kitchen, obviously a prisoner to his own woes.

Or maybe tonight our worries were one in the same.

I'd taken a cab the two miles back to my house, grabbed my car, and drove straight here.

I figured if anyone had the down-low on the details, it was Rex Gunner. He had connections in this town.

I'd also known him my whole life and trusted him implicitly. It was no secret he hadn't been the same since his wife had left two years ago, but the one thing that hadn't changed was his company's character. He saw to it that it stayed that way. And judging by the texts I saw, that hadn't changed.

I clicked open the door to my car and stumbled out, still reeling from my foolishness, barely able to stand beneath the crack in my heart. I'd allowed myself to be played. Hunted down like prey and ripped to shreds.

And God, those wounds burned and hurt and ached.

Because when I opened up, I opened all the way.

Reservations incinerated.

And that vile monster had gone straight for the kill.

I rushed up the walkway and quietly knocked at Rex's door so I wouldn't wake his daughter. It took only a second for me to hear heavy footsteps thudding on the other side, the twist of the lock, and the squeak of his door.

Rex jerked back when he saw me, blinking through his shock. "Lily. What are you doing here?" He widened the door. "Come inside where it's warm."

"Thank you," I managed, not realizing I was freezing, my bones chilled, my skin brittle as I rubbed my hands together.

"What's going on?"

Rex Gunner was every bit as powerful as Broderick Wolfe. But where Broderick went straight for what he wanted, disregarding anyone who got in his way, Rex kept himself barricaded by the hard scowl on his blatantly beautiful face, life hardening him to sharp edges and bitterness.

"I...were you working with Wolfe Industries on the Fairview Street project?"

Awareness dawned on his expression. "'Was' is the key word."

"I saw the texts you sent to Broderick," I admitted, lifting my chin, knowing full well what I was revealing. How else would I have seen them in the middle of the night? But I'd suffer any humiliation to gain the proof I needed to set my mistake right.

He looked to his feet, before forcing himself to look back at me. "You get yourself in some trouble, Lillith?"

"Only my heart."

With his hands on his hips, he gave me a tight nod, fully understanding.

"I need to know what you know so I can stop this. Addelaine Tindall was promised six months to relocate and one hundred and twenty-five thousand dollars to compensate her for the transition."

He huffed in anger. "I was told the same until I got word Addelaine signed a contract agreeing to a quick sale. Premises are to be vacated by the thirtieth and demolition begins on the first. RG Construction was supposed to have the bid, but I pulled it as soon as I got word. No question they have the city big dogs in their pocket because things just don't move that fast. Someone got paid off, and as soon as those types of dealings start goin' down, I'm out."

Anger and hurt billowed in my chest. "I can't believe he'd do this."

Rex eyed me. "Can't you?"

I pressed my hand to my mouth, trying to quiet the cry that slipped up my throat without my permission.

"Lillith," Rex murmured in sympathy.

I shook my head at him. "Just...tell me everything you know."

twelve

Broderick

Sunlight poured through the sheer drapes that covered the windows. I groaned as I stretched where I lay flat on my stomach, my muscles flexing as my cock stirred back to life, my body bristling with this desire I had a hunch wasn't ever going to lessen.

Just like I told Lillith.

Once I tasted her, I wasn't ever going to get my fill.

A satisfied grin stretched across my mouth, and I slid my hand along the mattress. Seeking her. Already ravenous. Ready for another bite. The only softness I found was the cool bottom sheet.

I jerked my head up from the pillow to look at the spot where I'd watched her fall asleep. The top sheet was gone.

So was she.

Anxiety twisted in my gut. "Lillith," I called, voice turned in the direction of the attached en suite bathroom.

Silence rained down, ominous in the still, quiet morning.

Dread seeped into my skin and settled in my bones. My gaze swept the room.

Her clothing, which we'd left strewn across the floor, was no longer there.

My teeth gritted. *What the fuck?*

I thought we were passed this.

I reached for my phone to call her, gripping it in my hand as I swiped my thumb across the glass.

The alarm I felt ratcheted up a thousand notches when I saw the messages that had already been read. My chest tightened in rage at what they implied. At the suspicions they confirmed.

Motherfucker.

Lillith had seen these texts.

God. I couldn't even imagine what she was thinking.

Panic spiraled through my body. My mind raced. Flipping through every detail James had fed me.

I flicked into recent calls listed on my phone until I found the name I was looking for.

He answered on the second ring.

"I warned you," I seethed.

Mocking laughter filtered in from the other end of the line, his disappointment thick. I shouldn't have been surprised. After all, that was the only thing I'd ever been.

"And I warned you. You had two weeks to get her out of there, not six months, and you sure as hell didn't have the authority to pay her what you promised. So I had my men fix it."

Anger rippled through my straining muscles. "I promise you, I won't let you get away with this," I said, crushing my phone to my mouth where I spat the words.

He laughed. "It's already done."

thirteen

Lillith

My head jerked up when the bell above the door chimed, flaming the indignant anger that burned through my body and trembled all the way to my core.

"Don't you dare walk through that door." The words shook and grated as I forced them through gritted teeth. Broderick Wolfe froze halfway through the door of Tindall's Thimbles. He was back to wearing his suit that made him appear every bit the villain he was.

Dark and dominant.

Last night, Rex Gunner had given me enough information so I knew where to begin digging. The proof I'd found in the few hours I'd spent combing through files on my computer was insubstantial, but hopefully it was enough that the complaint I filed to order a hold on the sale until the claims could be investigated would stick.

All night and morning I'd focused solely on this task. Refusing to give into the nagging thoughts of him. Thoughts of his touch and his kiss and the promise of something more. Refusing to let myself dwell on the fact that I'd been nothing more than a game.

A pawn used to bring down the final obstacle standing in his way.

The sickest part of it all was that obstacle was me.

He'd pitted me against myself.

He took the final step inside, and I narrowed my eyes at him. I guess I shouldn't have been surprised, should have I?

His throat bobbed heavily. "Lillith...I can explain."

Nervousness seemed to line his demeanor for the first time, but I knew better than to fall for his tactics. The man managed to switch from one disguise to another flawlessly.

That didn't mean I couldn't see his razor-sharp teeth.

"I don't want to hear anything you have to say." I lifted the short stack of papers. "I have everything I need to know right here. I know your company bribed the county commissioner. I know your company signed off on pushing the permits through. And I know your company had no intention of honoring the deal *you* made with Addelaine."

He rubbed a big hand over his jaw, which today was unshaven and coarse with thick, dark hair.

A beast.

A beautiful, terrible, lying, betraying beast.

Hate flared, that emotion mixed with the cutting grief.

"My father—"

Biting laughter broke through the air. "I don't give a damn about your father, Broderick. I give a damn about what you promised. What I care about is the fact you're nothing but a disgusting manipulator. A liar driven by greed."

I sucked in a sharp breath when he suddenly flew across the floor. He was in my face, nostrils flaring as he stared me down. Yet, when I expected to find anger in his eyes, I found nothing but desperation. His next words a hoarse plea. "You told me you trusted me. I demand a little of it now."

I refused the instinct to soften, and instead I scoffed as I tipped my head back so I could meet his penetrating gaze. "You *demand* it? You don't get to demand anything of me. You don't own me, and you can't have me. I promised you before you came here that I would stop you…but now? Now I promise I will destroy you. I won't stop until there's absolutely nothing left of Wolfe Industries. I trusted you, and you lied to me. Used me. And I fell for it."

The worst part was that I'd fallen for him.

Bile rose in my throat. "You disgust me, and I don't ever want to see you again unless it's in court and I'm taking everything important to you away."

He sank back, shoulders straightening as something like hurt flashed across his face. It was gone before I could decipher it, his jaw going rigid. "You really think so little of me?"

The words dripped like venom as they slid from my tongue. "I think even less."

What hurt so badly was I didn't want to. I'd wanted to think the best of him. Wanted him to be the man he'd shown me he was yesterday.

His lips pursed, and he nodded twice, as if he needed to accept what I'd said. Then he turned on his heels, strode toward the door, and pulled it open. He paused halfway out, looking at me from over his shoulder, his expression like a straight kick to the gut.

Pain.

"That's too bad, Lillith, because it only took three days for you to mean the most to me."

Then he tossed the door open wide and disappeared out into the glinting sun that shone through the frigid winter air.

I stood there gasping for air as I watched him go, trying to hold on to reason. To my senses and resolutions and the reality of who he was, all the while my spirit burning and aching, my insides twisting in two.

How had I let him hurt me so badly?

Off to the side, movement caught my attention, and I turned to find Addelaine wringing her hands where she stood in the archway to the sewing room in the back. "Child," she whispered like a loving reprimand.

Angrily, I swiped at the tears that started to fall when I saw her standing there. "He's a bad man, Addelaine. A big, bad man."

She shuffled forward, her head angling to the side as she did. "You didn't tell me."

I looked to the papers in front of me, pretending as if I could actually make out the words printed on the page through the bleariness that suddenly clouded my eyes. "There was nothing to tell," I said as offhandedly as I could muster.

She clucked in disapproval. "Lily, child. Come now. Do you think I don't know you better than that? That right there had nothing to do with this old building and everything to do with the expression you're wearing right now."

I jerked my attention back to her. "I made a mistake, Addelaine. A foolish, rash, horrible mistake, and because of it, I let you down. But I promise you, I won't fail you."

Addelaine peered up at me with her weathered face, and my breath caught somewhere in my lungs, my heart a tangle of pain and devotion.

This woman meant everything to me, and I'd let someone threaten that.

"Maybe it's a sign that we need to let this go. You've been fightin' a good fight, but maybe it's not the right fight. Maybe winnin' this one just isn't meant to be."

"How can you say that? You belong here. This is your home," I pleaded, pushing the papers that held the complaint across the counter toward her in a bid for her to sign them.

Her attention danced around her store like a loving caress. She turned back to me with a soft smile. "Yes, it's been my home." She tapped a finger at her temple. "But I hold the memories right here. And more importantly"—she tapped her fingertips over her heart—"I hold them here. And even if it scares us, sometimes change is okay."

She angled her head to the side as she reached out and set her hand on top of mine. "It's time you asked yourself why you're fighting so hard for this. You're no longer that girl who walked through my door lookin' for a place to hide. That girl needed walls to keep her safe. Are you going to continue to make her a prisoner to them?"

Tears clouded my eyes. I blinked, setting them free. "You know that girl was someone I never wanted to be."

She tenderly cupped my face, and even though I was much taller than she was, somehow I felt as if I was a little girl as I stared up at her motherly face.

"Yet, that girl is still a part of you, and she's always gonna be. She's important. She taught you the lessons you needed to know. She became the smart, successful, caring woman you are today. But she's also holdin' you back. Refusing to let you trust, even when the truth is right in front of you."

A frown twisted my brow, and I blinked rapidly. "What do you mean?"

A shot of air puffed from her nose. "You really think that man walked in here wearing his heart on his sleeve because he wanted to gloat about winnin'? If he did what you think he did, then he already won. That man came in here wearing remorse, plain as day."

My head shook, wanting to believe her so badly it vibrated in my spirit. But when I trusted, it only led to pain. "He's been foolin' us, Addelaine."

My words slipped into the casual tongue of my childhood, the hours I'd spent in this place sewing at her side, listening to her talk, strength growing each day as she instilled hope and belief in me.

"He's nothin' but a wolf in sheep's clothing."

She almost smiled. "Child, that man doesn't look nothin' like a sheep. Think he's wolf through and through. But I think he just might be your wolf."

"How…how could I ever believe him after everything?" I tossed the papers across the counter, the stack of them sliding and separating. "After I found all of this?"

Addelaine sighed before she began to shuffle through the stack of papers, pulling out the two different contracts she'd signed that were hidden beneath the stack of evidence I'd printed.

She pointed at the two signatures. "Look at this, child. Look closely."

Confusion knitted my brow while heartbreak trembled my lip.

She jabbed her index finger between the two of them. "Those signatures aren't close to bein' the same."

She looked up at me with a flash of fear in her grayed eyes. "And the men who came in here...they were...mean. Cruel and without compassion. I recognized it the second they stepped through my door. Just the same as I recognized the compassion in him when he first came here, too."

I blinked as I studied the signatures that were clearly different even though they both bore Brody's name. Broderick Wolfe III. A fact I had missed in my quest to find him guilty. In my mission to prove his betrayal, I'd overlooked the obvious.

Guilt built up inside me.

She lifted her chin. "You feel something for him?"

That feeling bubbled again. The affection and warmth I'd felt in his arms. The *possibility* that had become something tangible. I tried to resist it. Refute it. But it didn't matter. My own truth came flying out. "Yes. I feel so much, Addelaine. More than I should. It shouldn't be possible, but I do."

She smiled. "Then you need to ask him why you should trust him yourself. Give him a chance to explain and see where the heart leads. It's time for you to let it run. You've been holding it hostage for a long, long time. See what happens when you decide to *trust*."

The tears came unchecked, and I pressed my fingers beneath my eyes and wiped the moisture as I struggled for a breath.

"Oh God...I think I messed up."

In such a different way than I'd been accusing myself of all day. Because the thought of hurting him ripped me in two.

"What do you want?" she asked with a knowing smile threatening on her mouth.

Realization settled over me. Something powerful. Overcoming and overwhelming.

Unmistakable.

"Him. I want him."

Her smile bloomed into a full-blown grin. "Then go." Addelaine lifted my red coat. "Go, child, before it's too late."

I sat there stunned as I came to acceptance before I shot into action. Skidding around the counter, I darted for her, taking the jacket and dropping a kiss to her wrinkled cheek. "Thank you, Addelaine. For everything. I hope you know you mean everything to me."

She clutched my hand. "Same way as you mean everything to me. You're a good girl. Always have been. Now it's time for you to go get what you deserve."

Nodding furiously, I shoved my arms into my coat, wrapped the belt around my waist, and tied it as I flew outside. Cold air slapped me in the face, the sky an icy sort of blue. I didn't even slow. I just rushed down the sidewalk, winding through people who were on their lunch breaks, my heels clicking on the concrete as I stumbled along as fast as I could.

My heart thundered.

Heavy in my chest.

A pound, pound, pound as I let myself fully feel for the first time since I was fifteen. Without reservation. Without question.

Trust.

It was terrifying.

But freeing in the most miraculous of ways.

I moved faster, rushing across the street and heading in the direction of his hotel, praying he would be there.

That I wasn't too late.

That he'd give me the consideration I'd refused him minutes before. That he'd stop. Listen. Let me apologize. A frantic need built up, propelling me forward.

Faster.

Needier.

Filled with a hope unlike anything I'd ever felt before.

I gasped when I collided with a big body rushing my direction.

A stunning, powerful, strong body. Those big hands went straight to my face, gripping me tight, his eyes so intense and mesmerizing.

I clutched his jacket lapels. "Broderick...oh my God...I'm so sorry. I..." I forced myself to meet his steely intensity. "I told you back there that I fell for it, when in truth, I fell for *you*. That terrifies me, and the second something seemed to go wrong, I immediately thought the worst of you. And I don't want to be that person anymore. I don't want to be cynical and filled with doubt, always searching for the worst in people. Please…forgive me."

His thick throat bobbed. "Do you trust me, Lil' Redd?"

I swallowed hard, clutching his jacket tighter as I offered the words. "I told you I don't trust easily. I'm the one always waiting for the other shoe to drop. Just waiting on someone to let me down, because no matter how good things might be, they're bound to go bad. But it's time I realized I'm not that same girl who stood abandoned in that empty house. I'm not her. I've found love. A family. I don't have to be her anymore."

His hands cinched down on either side of my face. "I made both you and Addelaine a promise, and I intend to keep it. My father sent in his men to force this deal through and make it look like Addelaine agreed, threatening her into going along with it, and forging my signature to make me look like I was the one who was responsible. It's not the first time this has happened, but I promise you it will be the last. Tell me you trust me. That you believe I wasn't responsible."

My chin trembled when I nodded. "I do. Completely."

It was the truth.

Standing there with him, I'd never trusted anyone more in all my life.

Not with my heart. Not with my body. Not with *my* Addelaine and everything she represented.

He wrapped me in his warmth, pressing a bunch of kisses to my forehead, to my temple, to my lips, while my spirit soared. For the first time, freed.

He leaned back to meet my stare, his expression firm and unyielding. "I told you I always get what I want, Ms. Redd. I was already coming back for you. Because I'm not leaving this town without you."

I gazed up at him, my soul completely bared. "Then why don't you stay?"

A chuckle spilled from his mouth, and he hugged me tighter. "I think I like where this is going."

I breathed him in. At ease. Wholly. Completely. "I think I do, too."

He brushed back a stray lock of hair that whipped in the cold gusts of wind then threaded his fingers through mine. He lifted our entwined hands and grazed his lips across my knuckles. "Let's go, Ms. Redd. It's time to set things straight." He squeezed my hand. "Together."

epilogue

Broderick

"Do you think she's going to like it?" Her hopeful whisper tickled my ears as my Lillith stared out the window of Pepper's, a dingy old diner that just so happened to have the best pie in the entire town with a direct view of where Addelaine's building once stood.

Her raven hair cascaded over her shoulder. Her delicious, delicious shoulder. Fuck, I loved her skin. I loved her body.

And God, how much I loved the woman.

Finding someone like her hadn't been in the cards.

But we were never in control of the hand we'd been dealt.

I'd been dealt a straight flush.

Lucky me.

I couldn't stop the grumble of possessiveness that filled my chest when I looked at my fiancé, who was wearing that expression of careful tenderness that was at the true root of who she was.

I reached across the table and took her hand, brushing my thumb along the back of the silky flesh, wondering how that simple action managed to stir the hunger inside me. "How could she not like it? She's going to have primo space."

Tindall's Thimbles would be located on the first floor of the brand new hotel going up across the street.

She turned to look at me with a tiny smile. "You wouldn't have it any other way."

"Of course not. You love her."

Her teeth clamped down on her bottom lip.

So damned enticing. I wanted nothing more to be the one delivering that bite.

"And you love me," she murmured.

"More than anything."

I toyed with the huge diamond that glinted from her ring finger, the ring I'd given her just two weeks ago. The day we'd broken ground on the new hotel.

This woman had been instrumental in seeing to it that my father was stopped. His corrupt practices silenced in the evidence Lillith had worked nonstop to prove.

My father had resigned from the company, and I'd taken his place as CEO.

But I sure as hell wasn't walking in his shoes.

"Did you ever think when you came here that you'd stay?" she whispered.

I leaned her direction, inhaling her distinct scent, words a growl. "Not until the first time I tasted you."

She shifted in her seat, and a heated flush skimmed her flesh.

Affected.

Needy.

Ready.

Just the way I wanted her.

"Are you wet?" I murmured casually.

She not so casually nodded her head, a tremble raking through her body.

After pulling my money clip from the inside pocket of my suit jacket, I tossed a stack of bills onto the table.

Then I sat back with the challenge.

She clutched the table, a harsh breath parting her lips.

"Run, Ms. Redd. Because I'm going to chase you. And where

I catch you? That's where I'm going to fuck you."

She inhaled a sharp breath before she slid out of the booth, her knees clearly weak as she made her way through the restaurant. Today she wore a red summer dress, which she knew that color always drove me out of my mind, and a pair of sexy black heels. Her hair a black avalanche down her back.

She pulled open the door, only looking back at me to give me a smirk from her red, red lips.

Then she stepped out into the day and disappeared down the sidewalk.

I stood from the booth and straightened my tie.

The hunt was on.

And with her? It was never going to end.

the end

Thank you for reading *Hunt Me Down*! Did you love getting to know Broderick and Lillith? Please consider leaving a review!

I invite you to sign up for mobile updates to receive short, but sweet updates on all my latest releases.
Text "aljackson" to 24587
(US Only)
or
Sign up for my newsletter
http://smarturl.it./NewsFromALJackson

Watch for *Follow Me Back*, coming early 2018!

Want to know when it's live?
Sign up here: http://smarturl.it/liveonamzn

More From A.L. Jackson

ABOUT THE AUTHOR

A.L. Jackson is the New York Times & USA Today Bestselling author of contemporary romance. She writes emotional, sexy, heart-filled stories about boys who usually like to be a little bit bad.

Her bestselling series include THE REGRET SERIES, CLOSER TO YOU, as well as the newest BLEEDING STARS novels.

Watch for FOLLOW ME BACK, the second sexy, heart-warming romance in the new Fight For Me series, coming mid-2017

If she's not writing, you can find her hanging out by the pool with her family, sipping cocktails with her friends, or of course with her nose buried in a book.

Be sure not to miss new releases and sales from A.L. Jackson - Sign up to receive her newsletter http://smarturl.it/NewsFromALJackson or text "aljackson" to 24587 to receive short but sweet updates on all the important news.

Connect with A.L. Jackson online:

Page **http://smarturl.it/ALJacksonPage**
Newsletter **http://smarturl.it/NewsFromALJackson**
Angels **http://smarturl.it/AmysAngelsRock**
Amazon **http://smarturl.it/ALJacksonAmzn**
Book Bub **http://smarturl.it/ALJacksonBookbub**
Text "aljackson" to 24587 to receive short but sweet updates on all the important news.

Made in the USA
Middletown, DE
09 July 2019